THE PASTOR'S EASTER PRAYER

TINA RADCLIFFE

LOVE INSPIRED
INSPIRATIONAL ROMANCE

Special thanks and acknowledgment are given to Tina Radcliffe for her contribution to the Tumbleweed, Texas miniseries.

Recycling programs for this product may not exist in your area.

ISBN-13: 978-1-335-62145-0

The Pastor's Easter Prayer

For questions and comments about the quality of this book, please contact us at CustomerService@Harlequin.com.

Love Inspired
22 Adelaide St. West, 41st Floor
Toronto, Ontario M5H 4E3, Canada
www.LoveInspired.com

HarperCollins Publishers
Macken House, 39/40 Mayor Street Upper,
Dublin 1, D01 C9W8, Ireland
www.HarperCollins.com

Printed in Lithuania

Pastor Rob glanced around, his gaze finally returning to her.

"I'm feeling a bit dishonest at the moment. All the trouble you and everyone went to."

"You deserve it. Everyone was on board when I mentioned the idea."

"But..."

Hannah eyed him, confused. "What is it?"

"My birthday isn't until June."

She blinked. "The boys said it was coming up soon. Lucas was certain that it was this month." She paused. "Any day now, he said."

"June is soon. As opposed to December." He nodded solemnly. "I take full responsibility. I told them my birthday was soon as an excuse to go to the Friendly Fork for lunch."

She stared at him for a moment. Then she started laughing, unable to stop. Near to tears, she finally caught her breath. "Oh, my. And you played along."

"I saw the cake," he said with a laugh. "I was afraid you'd take it away. I mean, what a cake!"

"Yes. What a cake is right." Hannah smiled for a moment. Then reality hit. "Are we going to tell anyone about this?"

"Eventually." He glanced at her, his expression hopeful. "For now, can it be our little secret?"

"Our little secret," Hannah repeated. She liked the sound of that.

Tina Radcliffe has been dreaming and scribbling for years. Originally from Western New York, she left home for a tour of duty with the US Army Security Agency stationed in Augsburg, Germany, and ended up in Tulsa, Oklahoma. Her past careers include certified oncology RN, library cataloger and pharmacy clerk. She recently moved from Denver, Colorado, to the Phoenix, Arizona, area, where she writes heartwarming and fun inspirational romance.

Books by Tina Radcliffe

Love Inspired

Tumbleweed, Texas

The Pastor's Easter Prayer

Lazy M Ranch

The Baby Inheritance
The Cowboy Bargain
The Cowboy's Secret Past
The Cowboy's Forgotten Love

Hearts of Oklahoma

Finding the Road Home
Ready to Trust
His Holiday Prayer
The Cowgirl's Sacrifice

Big Heart Ranch

Claiming Her Cowboy
Falling for the Cowgirl
Christmas with the Cowboy
Her Last Chance Cowboy

Love Inspired Suspense

Sabotaged Mission

Visit the Author Profile page at LoveInspired.com for more titles.

Wherefore seeing we also are compassed about
with so great a cloud of witnesses, let us lay aside
every weight, and the sin which doth so easily beset
us, and let us run with patience the race
that is set before us.

—*Hebrews* 12:1

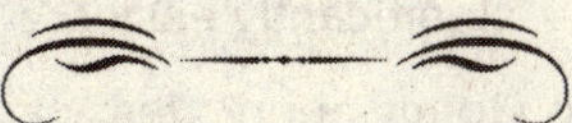

The release of *The Pastor's Easter Prayer* marks the 15th year I am releasing books of my heart with Love Inspired. What a humbling honor to have my dream of writing for this line come true. I am especially grateful to Senior Editor Melissa Endlich, for believing in me and gently pointing out that I needed to learn how to plot. I finally mastered that, making my life significantly easier.

Thank you to my agent, Jessica Alvarez, for her encouragement at all times.

Finally, thank you to the Love Inspired readers. You are loyal, devoted and kind. I am blessed.

Chapter One

Rob Sterling stared at the bulletin board in the Tumbleweed Community Church kitchen and chuckled. He'd been pastor here for six months now, and not a day went by without the church secretary, Hannah Bryant, posting a fresh motivational quote. Usually humorous. Often pointed.

Hopefully, today's quote wasn't indicative of her attitude toward her job. He and Hannah were the only full-time staff running the show. Everyone else, from the music director to the associate pastor and the custodian were part-timers or volunteers.

He laughed to himself. Who was he kidding? Hannah ran the show, and he'd be in a world of hurt if she left. Rob made a mental note to chat with her about job satisfaction.

Flipping off the lights, he began a routine walk through of the church before he left for the day. On Saturdays, he was usually the only one in the building. The peace and quiet allowed him to work on Sunday's sermon, and truth be told, avoid the world. A sad commentary for an appointed shepherd.

Tumbleweed Community Church was a small congregation that swelled to double their usual attendance at Easter and Christmas, depending on the weather. Friendly people, though he hadn't gotten to know them well quite yet. No rush, he'd kept telling himself. He'd promised local businessman

Jim Stewart—who'd lured Rob to Texas—that he'd give it until fall before he decided whether he would stay or head back home to New Hampshire.

Moving from the altar toward the back of the building, the sound of smashing glass grabbed his attention. Rob grimaced. Yep, that was a window for sure. As he raced down the aisle, past the glossy oak pews, toward the vestibule, his phone buzzed with an alert from the security camera app.

He pulled his cell from his pocket. It was a shame that a church needed a security system, but Tumbleweed, Texas, had the distinction of being the only gasoline stop off the highway between Houston and Beaumont. He'd been advised that strange occurrences were not unusual during tourist season when travelers detoured into town more frequently. Except it was the last day of February, a little early for tourist mischief.

The image on the camera took Rob by surprise. A young boy stood on the tree-lined walkway next to the church, by the employee entrance. He pulled a good-sized object out of his pocket and stared at the building. Winding up, he threw what looked like a rock. The kid had a good arm, he'd give him that. The rock sailed with purpose right through a high stained-glass window—an expensive, one-of-a-kind stained-glass window—before the boy raced off toward the park.

Rob grimaced when he reached the vestibule where, indeed, colored shards of the broken pane lay on the carpeted floor of the church's main entrance. He picked up the rock from among the ruby and emerald-colored glass pieces and tossed it in the air before tucking the offending weapon in his pocket.

What a shame. The stained-glass windows caught the sun each day and illuminated this foyer area in a multicolored shaft of light. The rest of the steepled, white church was unremarkable, but those windows…they were spectacular.

The playback feature on the security camera app allowed him to zoom in on the offender's identity. When he did, surprise had Rob jerking back.

Lucas Bryant. Hannah's son.

He knew the boy in passing, as the school bus dropped ten-year-old Lucas and his seven-year-old brother Noah off at the church at the end of the school day. Good kids, they'd quietly read or finish their homework in the church kitchen until Hannah was ready to leave for the day.

Backtracking through the church to his office, Rob sat down at his desk and called the custodian, Lester Harris, with a request to board up the window. Thankfully, though, tomorrow was March first, there was no rain in the forecast. He released a sigh and leaned back in his chair.

There was no way around this situation. He had to call Hannah.

Rob hesitated and adjusted his glasses. He'd never called her before, especially not after hours. The church secretary was so efficient, he'd never needed to. A tiny thing with wavy brown hair that seemed to have a life of its own and large brown eyes, she ran the day-to-day church business like a general. Hannah Bryant flat out amazed him.

Nothing missed her attention, which was a good thing, as his focus wasn't as laser-sharp as it used to be. Admittedly, he'd been in a fog since he lost his wife and their unborn child four years ago. The first year had been the worst. An entire year of his life missing. Since, he'd arrived in Tumbleweed, things had gotten better.

Still, each day was a battle against the guilt that attempted to consume him. Time and again, he reminded himself that he had two choices. Walk with the Lord or walk away. So far, he hadn't bailed on God, and the Lord hadn't bailed on him, either. Still, he had no idea what tomorrow's decision would be.

A walk of faith. That's exactly what he would have told a parishioner in crisis. So that was precisely what he told himself. Daily.

Take one step at a time.

Rob pulled up Hannah's number and pressed the green Call icon on his cell phone. She answered immediately.

"Pastor Rob, is everything okay?"

"May I stop by your house and chat with you about an issue?"

"My house? An issue?" She paused. "A church issue?" He heard the breathless panic in her voice.

"Not exactly."

Another pause.

"Okay, sure. I'm finishing up at the bakery. I'll be home in about an hour."

"The bakery?"

"Sweet Dreams Bakery. Across the street. I pick up a few hours here on Saturdays."

Hannah worked two jobs. Rob found himself nearly speechless. She was a single mother and had two jobs. Shame washed over him. For six months, they'd interacted on a near-daily basis. Why didn't he know this?

"We aren't paying you enough?" he finally asked.

"I have two boys and a mortgage. Juggling finances is never easy in the current economy."

This time, he paused, regretting his tactless question. "I'm sorry, that was out of line. Why don't I speak to the church board and see if there's room in the budget for a raise."

"That would be great."

Yeah, he agreed. The last thing he needed was to lose Hannah. "All right, then. If you could text me your address, I'll see you in an hour."

The ride out of Tumbleweed east toward Big W Ranch,

owned by the Wright Family, took Rob past lush land, where cattle grazed on the spring forage.

He easily found the turnoff to the dirt road that led to Hannah's home. Rob pulled off his helmet and swung his leg over his motorcycle. He glanced around. The house, a modest two-story white clapboard with green shutters, boasted a wide porch that stretched from one end of the front to the other. Empty terra-cotta pots sat on each of the porch steps, ready for planting. The house was surrounded by azalea bushes ready to burst with pink blossoms. To the left, a freshly painted picnic table and benches, between the house and a field, sat beneath the dense branches of an ancient American elm whose branches had only just begun to bud.

The place brought back memories of his grandparents' home in rural New Hampshire, though this property boasted dozens of loblolly pine instead of beech and hemlock.

Rob glanced to the right at the sound of a duck. In the distancc, a pair of bluebills coasted across a small pond surrounded by emerging daffodils. Next to the pond, a roughly hewn wooden fence surrounded a field where two horses inspected the ground cover.

The air carried a whiff of manure and the sweet scent of spring flowers. Spring came early to Texas. Back home in New England they were still shoveling snow in early March.

He smiled for no good reason other than appreciation of God's handiwork.

A screen door bounced on its hinges, and he turned to see his petite church secretary coming down the porch steps in jeans and a pink T-shirt with the bakery logo, and worn cowboy boots, her expression wary. Rob guessed Hannah to be in her early thirties, though right now she looked like a teenager. A cute teenager, he admitted.

Rob placed his helmet on the bike and walked toward her. "I didn't realize you owned a ranch."

She smiled. "I don't. I have a house in the country that borders the Big W Ranch. Patty Wright's land."

"I see horses."

"Nothing slips by you, Pastor." Hannah continued to grin, her sense of humor challenging his literal response. "Yes. There's a small stable where I board a few horses for folks for extra income."

A third job. "How do you manage to juggle all those balls?"

"Carefully. I moved out here after my…" Hannah glanced at the dirt and gravel ground, kicking at a stone with a booted foot, then back at him. "After my divorce two years ago. I want the boys to have all the benefits of living in the country."

An admirable plan. Tumbleweed was a terrific place to raise a family. He'd once thought the same thing about rural Humbolt, New Hampshire. Rob pushed away the memories. "Where did you move from?"

"Houston. But I spent a lot of time here in Tumbleweed as a kid. My grandparents had a farm nearby."

Rob nodded. He'd learned more about Hannah in five minutes than he had in six months. What did that say about his people skills? Not much. He'd spent way too much time in his head, he realized. That had to stop.

"Do you want to come in?" She thumbed toward the house. "Coffee will be ready in about five minutes."

His gaze skirted to the house, where something moved at the window. They were being watched.

"Are your boys home?"

"Yes. Noah comes to the bakery with me on Saturdays, while Lucas has chess club at the school. I picked him up and only just arrived ten minutes before you."

That explained the flour on her shirt and the askew bandanna holding her dark waves away from her face. He did his best not to smile at the disarray of his normally put-together secretary.

"Could we talk out here?"

"Sure. If this is about all those boxes in the workroom, I can explain. I've been collecting canned goods for the food drive the high school has every spring. I know the clutter can be a bit overwhelming, but this is for a great cause." She took a breath. "They'll be gone in a few days."

"Yeah. No problem. The food drive is a great project."

"So, you aren't here about the cans?" Confusion flickered in her eyes.

Rob fished his cell out of his pocket and tried not to sigh. He was about to complicate Hannah's orderly life, and he regretted what had to be done. "You should watch this," he said.

Horror slid across her face as she watched the video. It seemed clear she recognized the boy immediately.

"I'm… I'm…" Clearly rattled, Hannah stepped back, her hand covering her mouth. She nearly stumbled, and he reached for her arm, steadying her. "I'm so sorry, Pastor Rob." Tears welled in her brown eyes.

She looked at him from beneath a fringe of dark lashes. "You must think I'm a terrible parent."

"Not at all. Lucas is acting out. He's asking for help."

"Why didn't he ask me? I'm his mother."

"He's a kid. They don't always consider cause and effect. Not to mention hormones and emotions are sort of a mess at that age."

She cocked her head and assessed him. "Do you have kids?"

"Uh, no. No kids." He swallowed, pushing thoughts of the unborn child he'd lost when his wife died out of the way.

Hannah blinked. "Then how did you figure that out?"

Rob smiled. "You might not be able to tell, but I used to be a ten-year-old boy once upon a time."

A soft chuckle replaced the despair in Hannah's voice as she murmured, "Right." She paced back and forth, then stopped and looked at him.

"What am I going to do? Lucas won't talk to me about anything since the divorce. And lately, their father's visits have fallen to the wayside." Hannah cringed and crossed her arms. "I'm sorry. I hate drama. And here I am, giving you drama. It's enough that you spend so much time counseling parishioners during the week. You shouldn't have to deal with it on your day off."

"Not a big deal. Besides, we all have a little drama somewhere in our lives. Don't you think?"

"I guess so."

He offered his best reassuring smile. "Mind if he and I have a chat?"

"Not at all. I'm at the end of my rope here."

Minutes later, Lucas stepped outside, the screen door banging as he dragged his sneakered feet down the steps of the house and across the yard. A mop of dark curls bounced when he walked. He wore blue jeans and a white T-shirt with the logo of Tumbleweed Elementary School on the front.

Lucas's glance landed on Rob's motorcycle, and he paused, his gaze appreciative.

"Hey, Lucas," Rob called.

He nodded and approached.

"Have a seat."

The boy sat across from him at the picnic table, his attention glued to a knot in the wood. He didn't seem sullen or angry. On the contrary, Lucas appeared resigned to his fate.

"You've got quite an arm on you," Rob said.

The kid's head jerked up.

"Would you like to tell me why you broke the window?"

"How did you find out it was me?"

"Security camera."

"Oh." He first looked at Rob and then away, shame heavy on his shoulders. "I was mad."

"Mad about what?"

After a long sigh, Lucas met Rob's gaze. "Chess. I stink at chess."

"Chess." Rob pondered his response. "You're in fifth grade?" he guessed.

Lucas nodded.

"Why did you join the chess club?"

The boy reddened from his cheeks to the tip of his ears.

Confused, Rob stared at Hannah's son. His face only became redder. Then, the penny fell through the slot. *A girl.* He joined the chess club because of a girl.

"My dad said he'd teach me…" Lucas's voice wobbled. "But you know, he has a new baby and all."

"Why the church window?"

"I prayed for my dad to visit like he said he would." His head dropped as he said the words. "But he didn't. God's supposed to answer prayers, isn't He?"

"I know it can be hard to understand that God's timing isn't our timing and the answer to prayer comes in different ways."

Rob's chest tightened as a long silence stretched between them. It didn't escape him that, once again, he found himself dispensing advice on behalf of his heavenly Father. Advice he'd failed to take himself.

"About the chess," he finally said. "Maybe a friend could teach you."

Lucas raised his head "A friend?"

"Yeah. I could teach you."

Whoa! Rob nearly fell over when he realized what he'd

offered, but it was too late to take the words back. The boy needed to know there were men out there who followed through on their promises. Though he didn't consider himself a role model for anyone at the moment, like it or not, he'd just volunteered for a life lesson.

"You?"

"Sure. Why not? I happen to be an excellent chess player."

"You mean it?" He eyed Rob curiously.

"Yeah, I do mean it."

"Okay." The word was nearly a whisper.

"We still have a problem with the broken window."

A sick expression washed over Lucas's face. "I only have eighteen dollars and thirty-two cents in my piggy bank."

"There are consequences for our actions, Lucas."

The boy's face paled, the sprinkling of freckles across the bridge of his nose now evident.

"You and I will have to find a way for you to earn the money to pay for the window." Rob shook his head. "Stained glass. It won't be cheap."

"You mean, like a job?" Lucas pulled at the neck of his T-shirt as though he was being strangled.

"Exactly like a job."

"Doing what?"

"Good question." Rob narrowed his gaze as a tiny bubble of an idea began to grow. For weeks, he'd watched as Hannah filled the workroom with canned goods. He'd overheard chatter at the town diner about the food drive and how much it was needed.

Maybe the way to meet the needs of the flock was a year-round food drive. It didn't escape him that he had no clue what that would entail. But if the Lord put it on his heart, Rob trusted He would find a way to make such an undertaking happen.

At least if he left Tumbleweed after his agreed tenure ended in September, he'd be leaving the church in a better place than when he arrived.

"I'll think of something," Rob said to the boy. "In the meantime, I'll find out exactly how much a stained-glass window costs."

"And chess, right?"

"Yeah. I'll talk to your mother about how to fit that into both our schedules."

"I'm real sorry, Pastor Rob." Lucas swallowed. "It was dumb. I know it was dumb, but I wanted God to..." He shrugged and knuckled the moisture at the corner of his eye. "I wanted God to tell me why He didn't answer my prayers."

"Lucas, you're talking to the right guy. I get it. Not a day goes by that I don't want the good Lord to explain things to me. I understand. It's hard. Real hard."

Lucas nodded.

The tight, painful knot in Rob's chest only ached more. The hardest thing in life was living with so many unanswered questions.

He had more in common with this ten-year-old boy than he would have expected. Somehow, he had to find a way to ease both of their pain.

It was a tall order, to be sure.

Hannah stared out the window of her office at the view of the town square and smiled. March meant spring was on the way. Her favorite season. A time of restoration, when all things were made new. She recalled the first spring at the new-to-her house in Tumbleweed. What a surprise it had been when crocus and daffodils peeked out from the soft, greening land.

Green, like Pastor Rob's eyes behind his Clark Kent glasses.

Horrified at the direction of her thoughts, Hannah groaned to herself, turned on her computer monitor, and willed herself to focus on her mile-long Tuesday to-do list.

The very last thing she needed was more complications in her life. And Rob Sterling was definitely a complication.

The previous pastor had been pushing eighty and did not have broad shoulders that looked like he worked out, nor a swoony smile. Nope. And he definitely did not ride a motorcycle.

The fact that Pastor Rob looked like a cross between a football player and Superman's alter ego had not escaped the women of Tumbleweed, either. The first two months after his arrival, the casseroles and desserts came in bulk. Once word spread that the pastor was widowed, the influx only increased.

She doubted they'd bother to look in his eyes and see the one thing that gave Hannah pause. Pastor Rob was wounded. Not like an injured bird that could be rehabbed and freed to fly again. The man carried a profound burden.

Hannah had a penchant for trying to save the wounded. Look where that had gotten her. Married right out of college to a wounded man-child who dumped her eight years after their first child was born for a younger sales rep in his office. A woman who he claimed dressed up to serve the gourmet dinners she'd prepared and didn't fall asleep on the couch after the evening news.

Whatever. Hannah's idea of a Proverbs 31 woman did not include scrubbing a toilet in heels. So she prayed for the second Mrs. Bryant daily. Especially now that there was a brand-new baby in the picture.

The albatross was gone from around her own neck, and she was finally back in a good place, emotionally and spiritually, with the good Lord as the head of her household. With Him in control, life was good. Very good. Except for the whole, "more money going out than coming in" thing.

It was her boys she worried about mostly. Though she absolutely refused to bad-mouth her children's father, it was clear that Lucas and Noah were the ones being short-changed most from the divorce.

On top of that, she'd missed the warning signs that Lucas was unhappy. Pastor Rob seemed to figure out her child way before she had. That was a wake-up call. One that left her humbled and grateful for the intervention.

A tap on her doorframe had Hannah looking up, surprised to see Pastor Rob standing there.

The man was stealthy. Oftentimes, she'd realize he'd been at work in his office for hours, but she hadn't even noticed that he was in the building. Heat flooded her face, and she prayed he didn't read minds along with his other talents.

"Good morning," he said. As usual, he wore pristine jeans and a long-sleeved, starched Oxford shirt, sleeves rolled up, exposing his forearms. It was difficult not to notice how the pale blue shirt brought out the green in his eyes and emphasized his fit upper body.

"Good morning," Hannah returned. She handed him a stack of pink phone messages.

"Thank you."

"There are several counseling requests. I already scheduled them and synched the church calendar with yours. Patty Wright dropped off a casserole for you. I put it in the kitchen fridge. Looks like an enchilada special to me. Oh, and she said to let you know your sermon on Sunday was five stars."

He chuckled, fingering his glasses in a very Clark Kent way. "Mrs. Wright is overly generous with her stars and her delicious casseroles."

"That's not true," Hannah said. "I mean the stars, not the

casserole. Five stars is well-deserved. As for the casseroles, there are people in this town who covet Patty's casseroles and her pecan pies. The matriarch of Big W Ranch doesn't cook for just anybody."

"You're right. I'm honored and appreciative." He glanced at her. "So you agree with the five stars? I was concerned that I may have belabored the wonders of the kingdom of God."

"Not at all. It was excellent." She paused. "I group pastoral sermons into three categories. There are storytellers, or modern parable pastors, as I like to say. Then there are teachers. Those that provide clarity and understanding of Biblical history and theology. Finally, the fire-and-brimstone preachers. You are definitely called to be a teacher. I learn something new every week."

"Interesting theories," Pastor Rob said with a smile. His gaze locked with hers for a moment as though he was seeing her for the first time. "And um…thank you."

"Oh, I'm only telling it like it is."

"Your honesty is refreshing, Hannah."

"You say that today," she said with a laugh. Not everyone found her honesty to be a virtue.

Pastor Rob held up the pink papers in his hand. "Anything in here that's urgent?"

"No, but a Tom Archer called again and requested a callback."

Had she imagined it, or had Pastor Rob suddenly paled?

"Everything okay?" she asked.

"Yes. Absolutely. Tom is an old friend from back home." He cleared his throat. "Do you have a few minutes?"

"Sure. Is there another problem?" Her heart clenched. *Oh, please.* She hoped not. Seeing the plywood covering the broken window pane in the vestibule on Sunday had been a humiliating reminder of her parenting fail. Fortunately, Pastor

Rob hadn't shared with the community that Lucas was the one responsible.

"No. Not a problem. More like an opportunity." He moved farther into her office. "Do you mind if I sit down?"

"Of course not." Pastor Rob eased into the oak chair on the other side of her small desk.

"I'd like your help with a project," he started.

"Sure. I owe you plenty after stepping in with Lucas." She looked at him. "I still can't believe you volunteered to teach him chess."

He laughed. "You look doubtful. I'm actually a decent chess player."

"No. That's not it at all. I mean, your offer is extremely generous. I don't want to sound ungrateful, but…" Hannah faltered. "You meant it, right?"

"I did. I like chess. It'll be good for both of us."

"You're sure you aren't too busy?"

"Hannah, I understand what's at stake here, and I won't let him down. You can trust me, I promise you."

"Thank you," she murmured, relieved. "What about the window? Do you want to take it out of my salary?"

"No need. I have a plan to have Lucas work off the cost of the window. In the meantime, I'd like to contact the artist who did the work."

Hannah nodded. "I have all the information. Turns out she's local and a parishioner."

"You've already done all that?"

"We were closed yesterday, so I reached out to her. I'll leave the information on your desk as soon as I have a quote." She smiled. "So you mentioned a plan that involves Lucas?"

"Yeah. But not just Lucas. It involves the entire town." He hesitated for a moment, before meeting her gaze. "The Lord's put something on my heart. A church food pantry."

"A food pantry. Hmm. Sort of like a food drive year-round."

"Exactly. That's what inspired the idea. This town would benefit from a full-time outreach instead of only once a year. The problem is we're busting at the seams here in this building."

"What are you thinking?"

"I've noticed a few empty storefronts in town. Maybe there are more. You seem to know everyone, so I thought maybe you could do some reconnaissance to locate a budget-friendly spot for this idea." He glanced at the calendar on her wall. "If you'll make a list, call and get quotes. I'd like to launch this project immediately after Easter."

"Absolutely, I can do that." She jotted the information down, then looked up at him. "You mentioned budget-friendly?"

"Yes, a project of this size will mean putting the pantry on the budget request for next year. So when I say budget-friendly, I mean that we'd also have to find a way to fund the project ourselves for this year, and there's a lot of this year left."

We. She hadn't missed that word.

"I'm honored you've included me," Hannah murmured.

"That was a no-brainer decision, since you get more done in a morning than the Marines do all day."

Warmth washed over her at the compliment. "Thank you. I think."

"I'm only speaking the truth." Pastor Rob paused. "You have a lot going on in your life right now, Hannah. The pantry project is important, but I don't want you to take it home with you. Okay?"

She nodded, a little surprised that he understood how she functioned.

Pastor Rob stood, turned to leave, and then turned back. "Oh, and I like today's quote."

He chuckled as he left her office.

Hannah put her hands to her heated face as she recalled the words printed on a white square of card stock:

> Only grow thoughts on your brain that you wouldn't mind putting in a vase.
> —Anonymous.

The quote had been a reminder to herself to stop thinking about Pastor Rob.

Another fail.

"Get a grip, Hannah," she muttered.

He was her boss. Besides, the last thing she needed was another man in her life. A man with plenty of baggage, no less.

Relying on someone only led to disappointment when they let you down. And they always did. She'd learned that lesson the hard way from her absentee father and her children's dad. She was not ready to travel down that road again anytime soon.

Chapter Two

"I'll take a loaf of the sourdough and…" Hannah moved to the glass case of pastries, leaning close to examine the swirls of thick fudge on the chocolate cupcakes. She really shouldn't, but Luna Perez made amazing cupcakes and everyone knew it. Today was what the proprietor of Sweet Dreams Bakery dubbed Cupcake Wednesday. This was not the time for indecision. The treats would certainly be sold out by the end of the day.

"Four chocolate cupcakes, please," Hannah continued with a firm nod. She'd give one to Pastor Rob to thank him for his offer to mentor Lucas in chess.

"Do you think Pastor Rob dates?" Luna asked out of nowhere.

"Excuse me?" Hannah straightened with a start. Her gaze followed Luna's out the storefront window, where she stared with a wistful smile.

Tumbleweed Community Church was not the only church in town, but it did have the distinction of being the only church on the town square. The square consisted of a lovely park and gazebo in addition to the white steepled house of worship. Rows of storefronts lined Main Street, right across the street.

The bakery happened to provide an excellent view into the church parking lot, where Pastor Rob swung his leg over the seat of his motorcycle and removed his black helmet. Running a hand through his dark hair, he adjusted his glasses before heading into the building.

"Why? Are you interested in him?" Hannah asked. *Luna and Pastor Rob?* She shook her head. No way. Hannah knew her friend well enough to know that Luna preferred high-octane, adventurous men. Rob Sterling was far too tame for her. Hannah was not unhappy with that fact.

"Not at the moment, but you have to admit it's fun having a pastor who wears a leather jacket and rides a motorcycle. Tumbleweed has 'cool pastor' bragging rights."

"Fun?" Hannah murmured. Sometimes the ten-year age difference between her and Luna was more obvious than other times. Though she prided herself on being optimistic, some days the weight of her responsibilities made her feel much older than her thirty-five years.

"Pastor Rob reminds me of someone," Luna said. Tossing her long black braid over her shoulder, the baker narrowed her gaze in thought. "Like a superhero or something. You know?"

Hannah quickly glanced around the bakery. The cute, pink bistro tables with pink-and-black striped cushions strategically tucked around the room were empty. Thankfully, there was a temporary lull in activity now that the morning cinnamon roll rush had ended.

"Clark Kent," Hannah said softly. Not a superhero, but his alter ego. She'd given it a lot of thought over the last six months. Clark Kent. They were both in their mid-thirties. She couldn't verify Pastor Rob's age, but she was pretty sure. Six foot three and around two hundred twenty pounds. Idealistic, kindhearted and trusting. Always finding the good in others. Then there was the dark hair and glasses. Definitely Clark Kent.

"Yes!" Luna whirled around, grinning. "That's it. Does Clark Kent date?"

Hannah pointed to the bread. "Sliced, please."

Luna only laughed as she placed the loaf in the slicer. "You didn't answer my question."

"How would I know if he dates?" Hannah grumbled.

"You spend more time with the man than anyone else. For the last six months, to be exact. No one gets to Pastor Rob without the gatekeeper knowing. Come on. Don't you pay attention?" Luna slid the bread into a bag. "At least tell me what he's like."

"You go to church. You know what he's like."

"I mean outside of the pulpit."

"Luna, I've spent the last six months evading questions like that from his fervent female fans."

"Oh, come on. Give me some crumbs," Luna said.

"I don't know what to tell you," Hannah admitted. Yes, she worked closely with the man, but what did she truly know about him besides his preference for black coffee and a quirky sense of humor that often caught her off guard?

"Ginger over at the Beauty Lounge bought cookies here just last week," Luna said. "I heard a rumor that she put them on a plate and brought them to the pastor as if they were her own."

Hannah nearly gasped. She'd seen those cookies on the table in the staff kitchen with a note to "Help yourself" in Pastor Rob's handwriting stating they were from a generous parishioner. They were delicious, too. Now she realized Ginger hadn't made the cookies at all. It took all Hannah's self-control not to burst out laughing at how preposterous the situation really was.

"Is it true?" Luna asked.

"I can neither confirm nor deny that information." Hannah

waved a hand toward the cupcakes, suddenly irritated. "Four. No. Make that three. Chocolate fudge, please." She refused to join the Pastor Rob fan club.

"You're no fun." Luna retied the pink apron around her waist and opened the glass case.

"I'm not supposed to be fun. The pastor counts on me to be discreet. You know I can't gossip about the parishioners."

"Easy there, friend. I'm only kidding." Luna carefully placed the cupcakes in a pink-and-black striped box.

"Were you?" Hannah relaxed and let out a breath. "Sorry, Luna. You cannot imagine how many women in our community stop by the church to say hi and drop off food for Pastor Rob in any given week. It's beyond annoying the way they throw themselves at him." She slid her credit card across the counter to her.

"They say that food is the way to a man's heart, right?" Luna raised her brows as she ran the card through the reader and handed it back. "Maybe you should think about that."

"Seriously?" Hannah stared at her friend and then shook her head. "Don't even go there. And since you're into clichéd sayings, I will say I need a man in my life like a fish needs a bicycle."

"Oh, you're exaggerating. You're single. He's single. Why not?"

"First of all, he's my boss." Her boss with a couple of trunks full of baggage. Nope. Nope. Nope. "Second, I am not interested."

"Puh-lease." Luna groaned, dragging out the word like a piece of taffy. "If you give me that 'once bitten, twice shy' line again, I'm going to scream. Besides, maybe you should think about the boys. Noah and Lucas could use a role model."

Hannah flinched at Luna's mention of the boys. Yes, they could use a role model, and if and when the good Lord chose,

He'd bring one into their lives. Until then, they'd have to stumble along with their doting mother.

Tucking her credit card away, Hannah glanced at her phone. "Uh-oh, look at the time. Gotta run. Lunch break is almost over."

Luna's laughter followed Hannah out the door. She stood on the sidewalk for a moment, eyeing traffic on Main Street. As she did, a yellow sign in the shop window to the left of the bakery caught her eye. For rent? That was new. There used to be a watch repair business there. Or maybe a tailor. She couldn't recall, as it seemed the place was never open.

Hannah stepped back into the bakery.

"Miss me?" Luna asked with a grin.

"What's the story on the shop next door?" Hannah asked.

"That building has been empty for over a year. The owner lived in Colorado. When he passed, his estate was stuck in probate. Jim Stewart bought the shop. That sign only went up this morning."

"Doesn't Jim own your bakery?"

Luna nodded. "The bakery, the hardware store, and the grocery. The man has become an empire since he lost his wife."

"What happened there? It was before my time."

"Cancer. Jim and Linda were high school sweethearts right here in Tumbleweed. He lost her several years ago. Very sad. They were inseparable."

"How tragic." Hannah nodded slowly. "Thanks, Luna. You're better than Google."

"That's very true."

Hannah stepped out of the bakery again and peered into the store window. The only furniture seemed to be a long counter. Probably where there was once a cash register. A few boxes rested against one wall. Other than that, the place was empty. A clean slate, waiting for just the right business. She had a good feeling about this building.

Yesterday afternoon, she had called around, but there wasn't as much available in town as Pastor Rob had thought. Yes, there was a small space for rent in the building that housed the thrift shop. It had previously been a pop-up gelato shop with barely enough room for one or two customers at a time. She recalled the long line outside the store in the summers. The only other option was an empty building a few blocks off Main Street. It was not ideal as it needed work, and the square footage was more than a pantry required, equating to higher rent. And Pastor Rob had emphasized budget-friendly.

But this place…it was perfect. Hannah snapped a picture of the phone number in the window before she crossed the street and headed back to work.

Entering the side door of the church, along the path to the park, was the quickest route to the staff area. If she was very quiet, she could pass the pastoral offices and slip into her office without anyone noticing. The associate pastor and music director were chatty, and she needed uninterrupted time to compile a report on the rental properties, answer the morning messages, and prepare the church program for Sunday.

"Hannah, got a minute?"

She stopped and backtracked to Pastor Rob's office.

He greeted her with a smile, then sniffed the air appreciatively and glanced around. "I smell chocolate. Do you?"

"Yes. Cupcakes." She held up the box. "Would you like one?" The words popped out of her mouth before she could think better of the idea. Well, she didn't need the calories anyhow.

"Chocolate cupcakes?" He perked up. "Chocolate is my weakness."

"It is?" She cocked her head, confused. "That was generous of you to share those cookies you put in the kitchen."

"The oatmeal, coconut, and chocolate cookies." Pastor Rob grimaced. "Yeah, about that. Don't rat me out, please. I feel badly about the situation, but I'm not a fan of coconut."

Holding back a chuckle, Hannah smiled as she placed a cupcake on his desk. "It will be our little secret."

"I appreciate that. No need to insult parishioners." He appraised the cupcake before placing it on the credenza behind his desk. "My sweet tooth thanks you, Hannah."

"You're welcome."

"Before I forget, I'd like to schedule some time with Lucas." Rob shuffled the legal pads on his desk, pulled out a paper calendar, and flipped through the pages before looking at her again. The church leader was notoriously old school when it came to planners and calendars. "What do you think about after school?"

"Friday is a half day. Some sort of teacher training going on in the afternoon for all the Tumbleweed schools."

"Half day works for me." He glanced at his calendar. "I don't have any counseling scheduled. We can go to lunch."

"Are you sure you want to have lunch with a ten-year-old?"

"Absolutely. I like kids. They're honest."

"That is certainly true," Hannah said.

"I'll drop him off at your house in time for dinner."

Hannah frowned. "On your motorcycle?"

"No. I have a backup vehicle. Perfectly safe. Goes from zero to ten in thirty minutes."

She laughed. "That works. I'll let Lucas know."

"Does he have a chess set at your house?"

"No. He checks out a set from the school library to practice."

"I'll pick one up for our training sessions." Rob nodded. "I guess that's it. Thanks, Hannah."

"No, thank you, Pastor Rob. Oh, and I hope to have a report on your desk shortly regarding rentals and pricing." She paused. "Though you should know, there are only three possible locations. Out-of-town vendors have scooped up two others on my list. The summer season will be here before we know it."

"So I keep hearing," Rob said. "I'm thankful for the three you found. Any of those you're leaning toward?"

"The shop next to the bakery. Jim Stewart owns the place. It only came on the market this morning. Perfect size, and hopefully the perfect price."

His eyes lit up at her words, and he grinned. "Perfect location, too. I'll be praying we get the place."

Again, with the *we*, which was not a bad thing as long as she reminded herself that he was referring to the church community, not her specifically. Hannah averted her gaze. That would only be possible if she kept her eyes off the good pastor.

"Pastor Rob, Jim Stewart is here to see you."

Rob turned from the kitchen sink at the sound of Hannah's voice calling down the hall. "Be right there. Would you please have him take a seat in my office?" Rob rinsed out his mug and headed out of the kitchen.

"Yes, sir," Hannah replied.

He shook his head. After six months, she still called him Pastor Rob or the dreaded *sir*. The music director, associate pastor, and even the custodian all called him plain old Rob. Using his first name when he wasn't in the public eye allowed him to feel like he wasn't *on* 24/7. But maybe Hannah preferred that layer of formality. He'd have to ask her without somehow causing offense.

Pausing at the bulletin board, Rob read today's quote and smiled.

Find joy in every day. Not because life is always good, but because God is.
—Anonymous.

Hannah was spot-on. A merciful God who'd forgiven his trespasses. All that was left was for Rob to accept that forgiveness. He was well aware that he held on to the guilt of the past with a clenched fist, yet he had to admit that each day dawned a little brighter since he'd arrived in Tumbleweed, and his hand loosened a bit.

All good, and he had until September to decide if he was worthy of continuing in the pastorship role here in Tumbleweed.

Rob headed down the hall, whistling. Jim's sudden appearance had to be a positive sign since Hannah had only reached out for information on the property a few hours ago. Rob hoped he had a little sway with the man as it was Jim who recruited him to the position here in Tumbleweed.

"Afternoon," Rob greeted his friend and mentor.

"Pastor Rob. How's your day going?" Tall, with a full head of white hair, the former mayor offered a rare grin as he stood and shook Rob's hand.

"Joyful," he replied, recalling Hannah's quote. "You look like you're in a good mood as well." Rob gestured for his guest to have a seat as he slid into the chair behind his desk.

"I had ice cream with my granddaughter. She always makes me smile." Jim paused. "How are your folks?"

Jim was a friend of the Sterling family and often stopped by to say hello to his parents when he was on the East Coast visiting his own extended family. Rob was well aware that he owed the man much. Rob had floundered for several years after the loss of his pregnant wife in a house fire. He had finally accepted a position as an associate pastor in a megachurch in Raleigh. The position allowed him to remain in the background, something that suited him just fine at the time.

It was Jim who convinced Rob that he was needed in Tumbleweed. The call to return to the land of the living had been a life preserver.

"My folks are doing well," Rob said. "They're moving Gran into a care center this week."

"That's never easy."

"No, but she'll be closer to them and that means they can spend more time with her."

"Have you decided if you're staying in town come September?" Jim asked.

"Still praying about it," he said as he eyed the older man.

Jim nodded. "Prayer is good, but my intuition tells me that your time here is not nearly close to an end."

Rob fiddled with a pen on his desk as he tried to figure out where the conversation was headed. "It's not?"

Jim shook his head slowly. "Did you know that Abner Goldby will celebrate his birthday next month?"

"Um, no. I didn't." Abner Goldby. The name rang a bell, though he was certain that he hadn't been in for counseling.

"Abner will be one hundred years old. He's a World War II navy veteran." Jim paused for a moment. Then he went on. "There are less than sixty-six thousand of our Second World War vets left and the median age is ninety-nine. True heroes, those fellas."

"Yes, sir, they are. I had no idea about Mr. Goldby."

"And Maisy Jo Fromkin. She hit a milestone as well. Maisy Jo knit five hundred caps for the neonatal intensive care unit at Texas Children's Hospital." Jim offered a musing smile. "The hospital gave a reception in her honor."

"I didn't know that, either." He should have known. Would have known if he hadn't been standing in the shadows for the last six months.

Silence stretched between them for a moment before Rob cleared his throat. "Message received."

Jim nodded. "That isn't the reason I'm here. I stopped by because Hannah called about the property. I thought I'd check in with you and see why that particular building is on your radar."

Less than two hours ago, Rob had reviewed the information Hannah put together on the rental properties. Jim's shop was easily the best choice for the church's needs, as he was no doubt aware.

"I'm led to start a food pantry in Tumbleweed," Rob finally said.

"A food pantry." He looked at Rob for a moment, then gave a slow nod of approval. "I like it. Excellent idea and a terrific opportunity for you to really get to know your flock."

Ouch. Rob hung his head for a moment as the somber truth washed over him for the second time in fifteen minutes. "You're right. Very right."

A sly smile erupted on Jim's face. "I usually am."

Rob met Jim's gaze. "Does that mean you're interested in renting the property to the church?"

"I am." Jim hesitated.

"Why am I sensing a *but*?"

"Not a *but*—an *and*."

"Go ahead."

Crossing his arms, Jim said, "I'm always happy to participate in the Lord's work. However, I'm a businessman, and that means being a good steward of what He has tasked me with."

"I completely respect that," Rob said.

"I put that sign up this morning, and I've already had several interested parties inquire. I'll ask you what I've asked them. What's your long-term plan for the space?"

"Long-term *is* the plan. A once-a-year food drive isn't enough to meet the growing population and needs of the community. We need a permanent facility."

"Great. I require a one-year lease. However, I'm asking for the year's lease to be paid up front in lieu of a deposit."

"A year's lease?" Rob ran a hand over his face as the impact of the words hit him.

"Seems fair."

"Fair but problematic. You're on the church board. You know that the budget runs from July to July. Asking for that kind of money will be akin to pulling a rabbit out of my hat. And I don't wear hats."

"I'm open to negotiation. How does twelve months of rent for the price of ten sound? I'll throw in sixty days for free. What do you think?" Jim sat back in his seat with a benevolent smile, clearly pleased with the offer.

Rob eyed him. Was he purposely being obtuse? There were very few options. Tumbleweed Community Church ran on a shoestring budget as it was. A very short shoestring might be more accurate. Any funds borrowed from Peter to pay Paul would have to be recouped immediately.

"I think we need to call a board meeting to discuss all this," Rob admitted. "Are you doing anything tomorrow evening?"

"Thursday night? I guess I am now," Jim said. "And you're right. The sooner, the better. That property won't be on the market for long."

Rob would have laughed out loud at Jim's pressure tactics, except this was a serious matter. He needed that shop. How to make it happen was the question. "Let me reach out to the rest of the board," he returned.

"Sounds like a plan." Jim gave a nod as he stood. He fished in his pocket and pulled out two keys on a simple chain, dropping them on Rob's desk. "Here you go. Check the place out. I'll see you tomorrow night."

Scooping up the keys, Rob nodded. "Thanks, I will."

A moment later, after Jim had left, Hannah popped her head into Rob's office. The smile on her face faded when she looked at him. "Everything all right?"

Rob explained what happened. "Can you possibly be here for a board meeting tomorrow night?"

"Yes, sir. I'll get a babysitter."

"I'd hate for you to do that. How about bringing the boys along, and they can hang out in the kitchen? I'll order a pizza, and they can watch a movie on my laptop."

"You have a deal." Hannah smiled as she turned to leave.

"Hannah," he said. She did an about-face and met his gaze. "Would it make you uncomfortable to call me Rob?"

"I…um…" For some reason, she seemed flustered by the question.

"I mean, when we're not around parishioners. The rest of the staff does and it gives me the illusion that I can relax a bit when I'm not performing official duties."

"I never thought of it like that. You're right. I call everyone else by their first name. Rob, it is."

"You're sure?"

"Yes, sir." She laughed. "I mean, yes, Rob, sir."

He smiled at her gaffe. Then decided to seize the moment. "Um, Hannah? Do you know Abner Goldby?"

"Sure. Everyone does. He's going to be one hundred. Last year, he was honored at the state capitol with several other World War II veterans." She paused. "Why?"

"It came up in my meeting with Jim." He met her gaze. "I guess you know Maisy Jo Fromkin, too."

"Oh, sure. Did you see her picture in the *Gazette*? Maisy Jo was pleased as can be."

"Hmm. I must have missed that."

"Are you okay?" She cocked her head and looked at him. "Did Jim agree to rent the property to us?"

"He did. With a bit of a stipulation."

"Oh?"

"That's why I've called a board meeting." Rob opened his hand to reveal the key to the shop across the street resting in his palm. "The school bus won't be here for thirty minutes. Want to check out the place with me?"

"Absolutely, Pastor… I mean, Rob."

She followed him out of the building to the sidewalk. They quickly moved from the pedestrian crosswalk to the other side of the street, where Rob unlocked the shop door and held it open for Hannah. The electricity was off, but swaths of sunlight managed to sneak into the space through the dusty window, illuminating the front room.

Rob's spirits lifted as he scanned the rental property. The place was a step back in time. It could have been a candy shop or a millinery. Tin tiles adorned the ceiling, along with detailed oak trim. One wall was entirely faded brick, while more of the detailed trim work adorned the oak window casings and the long freestanding oak counter in the center of the room. Two of the walls were white-washed and needed a paint job. A fourth wall had been covered in now peeling, striped wallpaper, which would have to be removed. Still, not too bad for a shop that had been sitting empty for over a year.

He could envision the words *Tumbleweed Community Church Pantry* stenciled on the front window. Excitement stirred in his spirit.

"Oh, this is much better than I thought," Hannah said. "All we need is paint and some shelving." She stepped through a door that separated the front from the back room. "Lots of storage back here. We'll need better lighting, though."

"What do you think about asking local businesses to sponsor us?" he asked. "Like they sponsor baseball teams."

Hannah whirled around, her eyes bright with excitement. "Absolutely. There are plenty of sponsorship perks to be had. I'm thinking a banner to hang outside the store with their logos front and center, and shopping bags with their company name."

"Those are great ideas," Rob said. "You have a natural marketing mind."

"I actually have a degree in marketing. When I lived in Houston, I worked with a small marketing and publicity firm."

"You're underutilized in Tumbleweed. Why are you working at the church?"

"Because I want to live and work locally. Work-from-home options still require me to commute to the city a few days a week. I'm not interested in leaving Noah and Lucas for long stretches."

"I admire your dedication to your kids," Rob said. "And I'm happy we have our own marketing specialist at the church." He chuckled. "Now our biggest obstacle is financing, since Jim wants ten months of rent up front. Pardon the reference, but that will definitely take some divine intervention."

Hannah's lips curved upward. "Isn't it fortunate that we have a direct line to Him, then?"

Leave it to Hannah to cut through to the heart of the matter. "Yes," he finally said with a smile. "Yes, it is."

Chapter Three

"I don't see why we can't issue a short-term payment to cover the pantry building lease," Patty Wright said. The wealthy owner of Big W Ranch had all eyes on her when she spoke. At sixty-five, the petite widow carried serious clout in the community. She was a prime example of Texas proud. Though her son Ben managed Big W Ranch, Patty kept her hand in the day-to-day operations. Every now and again, she'd ride the fence lines that bordered Hannah's yard and give a wave to say hello. A godly woman with a good deal of sass, and Hannah looked up to her.

The church conference room was full. Hannah looked around the table at the four board members in attendance. Everyone had managed to make it to the hastily called Thursday evening meeting except the board secretary, Dixie Jarrett, who was also the editor of the *Tumbleweed Gazette*. Her daughter was busy giving birth, so Dixie was at the hospital and Hannah had agreed to take notes.

This was the first time she'd been privy to a board meeting, which both honored and terrified her. The church board consisted of the town's most prominent leaders, people whose decisions impacted the town in a big way.

"Short-term payment?" Jim Stewart looked at Patty like she was a steer with two heads. He crossed his arms and frowned. "That would be highly irregular."

"Oh, lighten up, Jim." The words came from Louise Mitchell, board president and Tumbleweed's current mayor. She patted her bouffant and well-shellacked, closer-to-God, silver hair. "Unemployment is up everywhere, including in Tumbleweed, and I have the stats to prove it. There are many people in this community who would benefit from a pantry. Let's find a way to make this work instead of focusing on 'irregularities.'"

Hannah hid a smile. Louise loved to share statistics and did so with the ease of an auctioneer at a cattle sale, which was probably why she beat Jim in the last mayoral election. Her constituents were bored by stale rhetoric, but numbers—numbers impressed folks.

"I agree," Patty said with a nod to Louise. "Our mission has always been to meet the needs of the community."

Jim arched a white brow. "I think the reference was about spiritual needs."

"You're being a grump again, Jim," Louise warned. "The church is the core of this community. If we can feed the flock physically, then we should be willing to do so. Hard to focus on your prayers when your stomach is grumbling." She turned to Patty. "What did you have in mind?"

Patty looked across the table at Ron Garcia, the Tumbleweed High School principal who was also the church board treasurer. "Ron, what about a ninety-day advance to cover the lease? I don't recall the budget numbers from last month. Can we cover something like that?"

"Our numbers are right on target. We could definitely do that as long as the loan is paid back in ninety days." He looked around, his gaze landing on Jim. "If everyone agrees."

"I'll go with the majority," Jim said with a shrug.

A quick vote approved the plan and Hannah's encouraging gaze met Rob's. He adjusted his glasses. A sure sign he was still anxious about the situation.

"Ninety days to pay back the loan." His expression said he was wrestling with the decision. "How will that happen?"

"There's nothing we do better in Tumbleweed than fund-raise," Patty said with a wink.

"True enough," Louise concurred. "Why, Pastor Rob, this is well before your time, but two years ago, we raised money for repair work on Johnny-Ray Fisher's house. Poor fella lost everything in a fire. We raised enough to fix his house and buy him a second-hand pickup truck."

"Wow," Rob said. "That is an amazing story."

"It's not a tall tale, either," Louise said.

Hannah recalled that fundraiser. She had moved to Tumbleweed around that time. She also remembered the details. It had taken an entire summer to raise the money. They didn't have an entire summer.

"Excuse me," Hannah said with a glance around the table.

"Yes, dear," Louise said.

"I thought I should remind everyone that the Tumbleweed Days committee will be knee-deep after Easter, which is four weeks away. That means we actually have thirty days to raise the funds because whatever we decide needs to happen before Tumbleweed Days."

"Oh, my. You are absolutely correct. All eyes will be on our biggest event of the year," Louise agreed. "There's no time to fiddle around. We have to put it in gear, folks."

"Do you have any ideas, Hannah?" Patty asked.

"Rummage sales are always lucrative fundraisers. The key is to keep the overhead low. Since we can use the church parking lot, advertising will be the only cost. Everything else should be solicited from the generosity of community members. In fact, the more community involvement, the higher likelihood of success."

"She's right," Louise said. "Folks like to give back. Growth for charitable giving is up one hundred and eighty percent in the last ten years."

"I didn't know that, Louise," Rob said.

Louise beamed. "Absolutely true. We should capitalize on that."

Jim tapped his fingers on the table to get everyone's attention. "Just a minute there. Are you talking a garage sale?" He shook his head, clearly unimpressed.

Hannah sat up straighter in her chair and avoided Jim Stewart's critical gaze as she responded. "A rummage sale put on by the church would be much more expansive. But, yes, it would be a garage sale on steroids."

Taking a nervous breath, she continued. "You've heard of spring cleaning, right? Folks clean out their closets this time of year. That will provide free inventory. Inventory that's tax-deductible for those who donate."

"I like the idea," Louise said. "I like it plenty. I'll be first in line, too. I have an attic filled with stuff I've been meaning to get rid of. And if my husband goes fishing that weekend, I'll empty out the garage as well." She belly-laughed, her beehive hair wobbling as she did. "Won't he be surprised?"

"What if it rains?" Jim asked. "Texas weather in the spring is mighty capricious."

"We could move to the high school gymnasium as a backup in case of bad weather. Won't be easy moving all the inventory, but at least we'd have a free option," Ron Garcia said. "I'm sure the school board will approve of such a worthy cause."

"Does that answer your 'glass half-empty' concerns, Jim?" Patty asked.

"For now," he muttered.

Just then a phone rang, and Rob pulled his cell from a pocket, glancing at the screen. "Would you excuse me for a moment?"

As soon as he left, Patty turned to Jim. "Why are you being so pigheaded about this? Making him pay a year's lease up front? That seems unusually challenging. What's the point?"

"Ten months, not twelve. I offered him a discount."

Patty rolled her eyes.

"Look, I have my reasons," Jim said. "Y'all are going to have to trust me. I know Rob Sterling well, and this arrangement will benefit him, the church, and ultimately, the entire community."

Hannah thought about Jim's cryptic words, uncertain what he meant.

"I am willing to trust you, since you are responsible for bringing Pastor Rob to Tumbleweed in the first place. Points for that," Patty responded. "However, let me be clear. I plan to do whatever I can to make this project a success. This project is bigger than our pastor—surely you can see that."

"I can," Jim shot back. "But do you really believe a rummage sale can raise enough money to repay the loan?" Jim's skeptical tone matched his expression.

Hannah cringed at Jim's blunt assessment.

Rob walked back into the room, his gaze ping-ponging from Jim to Patty.

"Yes, and I'll put my money where my mouth is," Patty said. "Big W Ranch will match whatever is raised." She gave Jim a pointed look. "I challenge you to do the same."

"I can do that, but I put the challenge back in your court," Jim said. "How about parting with a few of your blue-ribbon pecan pies as well."

Patty frowned. "My pies? What on earth do you mean?"

"How about selling those pies of yours. Cans of food donated to the pantry to purchase your pies."

Patty laughed long and hard. "I'll be happy to put my pies where my mouth is." She offered a coquettish smile. "That's a very clever idea, Mr. Stewart."

"I thought so." Jim leaned back in his chair and crossed his arms, looking very pleased with himself.

Rob's gaze moved to Hannah, and his lips twitched. The subtle flirtation between Patty and Jim hadn't gone unnoticed by the pastor, either.

"All right, then." Louise looked at Rob and Hannah. "The Tumbleweed Ladies' Auxiliary meets on Sunday evening. I know that doesn't give you much time, but if you provide us with a list of things we can do to help, we'll get right on it."

"I appreciate that, Louise," Rob said. He turned to Hannah. "Anything else?"

"Advertising is our top priority. I'll get an ad in the Monday *Gazette.* All the details will be in the Sunday church bulletin, as well. Of course, we'll need flyers in all the local businesses."

"Email me a file, and I'll get them printed up," Louise said. "The ladies can pass them out around town immediately."

"That would be perfect," Hannah said. Excitement simmered as the rummage sale started to gallop into reality.

"Big W Ranch will donate funds for a street banner," Patty said.

"Now, hold on there a minute, Patty," Jim protested, sitting up straight in his chair. "Stewart Properties is happy to donate as well. There's room for both of us on that banner."

She cocked her head and looked at him. "Is there?"

Jim opened his mouth and closed it, flustered by her response.

Louise started laughing. "Well, I'll be. Mark the date and the time. Jim Stewart didn't have a comeback."

"Getting late, folks," Ron said, stifling a yawn. "And I've got an early meeting tomorrow." He turned to Rob. "I'll get that check to your office to co-sign sometime tomorrow."

"Thanks, Ron."

"No, thank you, Pastor Rob. The pantry is God-given inspiration, and I'm happy to participate. I don't have the funds of my friends here, but I'm handy with a staple gun and willing to provide plenty of sweat equity."

Rob smiled. "We'll remember that. Thank you."

Ron hesitated as if he had something on his mind. He inched closer to Rob and lowered his voice. "I keep meaning to ask what happened with the stained-glass window."

Hannah couldn't help but overhear the conversation. She practically dug her nails into her clasped hands as she focused on her yellow legal pad and waited for his response.

"An accident." Rob shrugged. "Not a big deal."

"Will you need to use discretionary funds until the insurance claim is settled?" the principal asked.

"No need. I've got things under control."

Ron nodded and gave the pastor a wink. "I leave it in your more-than-capable hands, then."

"I appreciate that."

Grateful for Rob's answer, Hannah released a breath, her gaze on the church board members as they left the room, chatting amongst themselves.

She was all for Lucas reaping what he sowed, but this was a small town and once you were labeled as a troublemaker, folks had a hard time forgetting. Rob had given her son a precious gift. Grace.

Hannah wouldn't soon forget that.

"You okay," Hannah?" Rob asked. He eyed her as he gathered his papers from the conference room table. She tucked in chairs quietly but hadn't said a word since the board members had left.

"Thank you for your response to Ron about the broken window."

"No need to thank me," Rob said. "I recall an incident when I was Lucas's age. He's in for a wake-up call and some pain, but the lesson will stay with him for a long time."

"Still—I appreciate your discretion. Let me know how much the window costs and I'll reimburse you."

"That's not necessary," he said. "I've worked out a deal with Lucas."

"Yes. I get that, but the funds have to come from somewhere."

"Tell you what. If I need money, I'll let you know, okay?"

Hannah frowned, clearly not pleased with his answer.

"As for the rest of the meeting," Rob continued. "I may have bitten off more than I can chew. It's highly likely that my ego got in the way, too."

"What do you mean?" Hannah picked up a pen from the carpet.

"This community means a lot to me. I want to prove myself worthy of the chance Jim Stewart has given me. I wasn't really living when Jim approached me. Merely going through the motions. It's taken time, but lately, I feel like I've woken from a long sleep." He glanced at Hannah, "I agreed to a one-year contract here in Tumbleweed. I want to leave the town in a better place than when I arrived. The food pantry is a way to do that."

"What? Jim never said anything about a one-year contract." Her eyes went wide. "So, you're leaving in September?"

"That's the plan, though I haven't felt any direction about what's next. The community pantry is the only thing I feel strongly led about." He nodded toward the door and turned off the lights. "Though I'm willing to admit that I could be way off base. Once again, I'm concerned it may be my ego that's pushing for something that isn't meant to be right now."

Hannah followed him out of the room to his office, her legal pad tucked under her arm.

"While the pantry is a way to give back to the community, a ninety-day loan is a huge risk. Not only for me, but for the entire church. To tell you the truth, I'm stunned the board even approved the plan. I don't know, Hannah. I suspect I've forged ahead faster than I should have."

"I disagree. You know how you get that discomfort when something is off and the peace that you feel when it's right?"

Rob nodded. He definitely understood what she was saying.

"I have peace about the pantry," Hannah continued. "For what it's worth, I don't think your ego is in the mix. You've had a great idea. It's not a golden calf. This is for the community. Yes, it will be a challenge but anything of importance is. We can make this work."

"Can we?" He shook his head as he rounded his desk and sat down. "Don't get me wrong. I think the rummage sale is a great idea. Though, admittedly, the project is way outside of my expertise. I don't know how to ensure that a rummage sale is successful."

"But I do." She grinned.

"Says Hannah of the three jobs. I can't ask you to take this on as well."

"It'll be over in a few weeks."

"Yeah, that's the part that scares me. Even if we do raise the funds, we still have to prep the pantry and stock the place. Though that is definitely where your son comes in."

"Lucas will be helpful, but this project is all about two words. Volunteers and delegating."

"Do you think we can find volunteers to manage the place once we launch?" he asked.

"Absolutely. Which reminds me, have you talked to Sam yet?"

Rob nodded. The associate pastor was usually on board for anything as long as it didn't interfere with the pursuit of his postgrad theological degree. "I spoke to him last night. He's got a busy schedule but promised to rally the youth group to get the word out. He suggested a youth car wash with canned good donations for the pantry."

"There you go," Hannah said with a flip of her hand. "You already have an army at your disposal."

"I plan to sign up to volunteer in the pantry. I can fit in a few hours on Saturdays. In fact, I can bring Lucas with me after his chess club, if that works."

"That would be great." Hannah paused. "Remember, Louise did volunteer the ladies' auxiliary. I can promise you that once they find out you're going to be present on occasion, they'll be fighting to be first in line, like a dollar sale at the Grocery Spot."

"Really?" Rob narrowed his gaze, confused by her answer. "What makes you so sure?"

Hannah laughed, mirth sparkling in her dark eyes. "Are you kidding?"

"Kidding? About what?"

"Pastor… I mean, Rob, this town has a ratio of five women to every one man. Louise can verify that stat. You've got a respectable job, you're not on the FBI's Most Wanted list, and you aren't hard on the eyes." She grinned. "Mark my words. They'll be lining up."

Was that a compliment? Unsure how to respond, especially the not-hard-on-the-eyes part, Rob looked at Hannah. If it was a compliment, he'd have to return the favor. If things were different, he'd be interested in the church secretary romantically. She was smart, savvy and attractive. But things weren't different. He was a guy whose track record led him to believe he wasn't worthy of someone like Hannah.

"What do you think?" Hannah asked.

He nodded, realizing she was still talking, and hoping he hadn't missed anything important. "I'm sorry, I missed that last part. I was thinking about the pantry."

"I said people with goals are ten times more likely to succeed."

"You've been hanging out with Louise, our illustrious mayor and resident statistician, haven't you?"

Hannah laughed. "No, I read it in the *Gazette*."

Rob laughed along. Then he got serious. "Our goal is to raise a year's rent in two days. I wonder what the stats are for pastors agreeing to impossible goals." He ran a hand through his hair. "Don't get me wrong, Hannah. I like your rummage sale idea, but we're going to have to bring in an incredible amount of donations that will translate to cold, hard cash." He shook his head. "What was I thinking?"

Ignoring his comment, Hannah sat down and flipped to a clean page on her pad. "Let's write down our goals and a plan to achieve them." She scribbled quickly. "First we determine the days for the event and the hours."

"Right before Easter week." Rob pulled out his calendar and stared at the dates. "Yep. Friday and Saturday. March twenty-seven and twenty-eight look like our best option."

She jotted on the paper. "What about event hours?"

"What do you suggest?"

"The cool of the morning and not too long a day. That way folks feel a bit of urgency to buy."

"Eight a.m. to two p.m.?"

"Perfect." Hannah nodded. "We'll need a drop-off point. That's going to be challenging. We can start with the work area and the storage room, now that the food drive is over."

"How about the choir room?" he asked. "We can move rehearsals to the chancel if we end up needing an overflow space."

"That works, though Henry will not be too happy."

"We're all going to have to be flexible," Rob said, knowing Hannah was right. Henry Mattigan was a bit set in his ways, and the Easter services were the retired music professor's crowning achievement. Rob grimaced. The situation would take some significant finesse on his part.

"What about pickups?" Hannah asked.

"Pickups? Like a pickup truck?"

Laughter spilled out from Hannah. "Picking up donations in the church van."

"Sorry, I'm getting tired. Today has been a long day." Rob chuckled. "What kind of license does that take?"

"The van only seats twelve so it's a regular Class C. I can drive—"

"No." He raised a hand. "You said delegate. That means you aren't going to do everything. Okay? I'll figure out the van part."

"Yes, sir." Hannah saluted. "Anything else, sir?"

Rob laughed. "No. You better get those boys home. Thank you for all your help tonight."

"That's my job." She smiled. "See you tomorrow."

"Tomorrow," Rob murmured. He studied the calendar again, counting the weeks until Easter.

Four weeks.

Yeah, if one thing had been made clear tonight, it was that he was about to undertake one of the biggest challenges of his life. Rob also knew that if the good Lord had dropped the inspiration for the community pantry into his heart, He would find a way to make it happen no matter how impossible things appeared on the outside. And they sure looked impossible.

"Well, Lord," Rob said softly. "Once again, I'm trusting You."

Chapter Four

On Friday, Rob stepped into the church kitchen and headed to the coffeepot. Across the room, Hannah stared out the window at the town square, her back to him. She adjusted the collar of her blouse and smoothed her dark skirt nervously.

"The school bus should be here any minute now," she said. Frowning, she glanced at her phone and then back out the window.

"Have you got to be somewhere?" Rob asked.

Hannah whirled around. "Oh, sorry. I was talking to myself. I didn't realize I said it out loud." She shook her head. "Have you always been so stealthy?"

"Am I?" He cocked his head. Maybe so. He'd lived alone a long time, and spending so much time in house of the Lord required a certain level of silence.

"Yes."

"I'll work on being noisier."

"That would be helpful," she said with a chuckle. "And, yes, I have an appointment with Dixie Jarrett over at the *Gazette*. She's only in the office half a day today, because of her grandbaby's birth and all. I want to get that ad in the paper before the next issue comes out."

He nodded and put a hand to the coffee carafe.

"The coffee isn't hot," Hannah said. "Sorry. I unplugged the pot."

"Don't worry. I like it cold." Rob cocked his head toward the door. "Go. Noah can hang out with me and Lucas."

"Are you sure?" She grimaced. "I hate to impose on you even more."

"You aren't. I've been looking forward to today." He filled his mug with coffee. "In fact, I'm springing for lunch. Happy to have Noah join us."

"What? Why would you do that?"

"Mostly because I'm starving. But also because you've given above and beyond to this job and I've only been a placeholder."

Hannah opened her mouth to respond, but Rob held up a hand. "And because starting Sunday, things will no doubt be a little busy around here, and it won't end until the rummage sale is over. Learn to accept help, Hannah. We're a team."

"But… Noah and Lucas and lunch?" Her expression remained skeptical.

"Not a big deal. You do it all the time."

"Yeah, but I'm their mom."

"And I'm their friend. We've shared cookies and milk after school for over six months." He paused. "Please allow me to do this, Hannah."

She hesitated. "If you're sure…"

"I am." He took a long swig of cold coffee. "Oh, and we're going to visit the stained-glass artist's studio. Paying restitution for a window is abstract. Seeing what goes into creating the art will have a longer-lasting impact on Lucas."

"That's a life lesson you're talking about. Excellent plan."

A moment later, Noah and Lucas burst through the church's employee entrance and thundered down the hall and into the kitchen, laughing.

Hannah wrapped an arm around each of the boys and

kissed the top of their heads. "I've got an errand to run. Be good for Pastor Rob."

Noah glanced from his mother to Rob his face lighting up. "I get to stay with you, too?"

Rob looked at Lucas. "Is that okay with you?"

Lucas nodded.

"Great." Rob waved to Hannah as she left. He downed the rest of his coffee before placing the mug in the sink.

"I thought we were going to play chess," Lucas said.

"We are. After our field trip. Today is officially guy's day out," Rob said. "First, we've got to find sustenance. Any ideas where?"

"The Friendly Fork has the best burgers in town," Lucas said.

"You've had their burgers?"

"Mom says we're on a budget. We only get to go on my birthday," the boy said.

"Good news. It's almost my birthday and I want burgers and fries today."

"Yay!" Noah grinned and clapped his hands.

"When's your birthday?" Lucas asked.

"Soon enough," Rob said. He glanced at his phone. "We should get going. You can leave your stuff in your mom's office but take your jackets. I'm going to grab mine, too."

"Are we riding on your motorcycle?" Lucas asked, his eyes widening.

"Only if I want your mother to ground me. We can walk to the diner and then I have a surprise field trip for you." He tossed his keys in the air. "We'll take my car for that."

"Aw," Lucas groaned. "I wanted to ride on your motorcycle."

"Yeah, that's not happening. Moms know best. Meet you in the parking lot."

Minutes later, Rob led the boys across the street. They passed the bakery, which was closed for the day. A few steps away was the Beauty Lounge. When several ladies in the window waved at them, both Lucas and Noah giggled.

"What's in their hair?" Noah asked. "It looks like tin foil."

"They're aliens," Lucas said.

Rob laughed and offered the women a wave in return. "I'm clueless about what goes on in there."

They stopped in front of the Friendly Fork Diner, where Rob held the door.

Country music rang out from a juke box in the corner, an accompaniment to the buzz of voices in the crowded establishment.

"Why, Pastor Rob, as I live and breathe." Rosie Foster, the diner's manager called out from behind the front counter. "So happy to see you in our humble diner." She approached them with menus in-hand and a pencil protruding from the blonde bun at the top of her head.

"Thank you, Miss Rosie," Rob returned. "We're having a fellas-only lunch today."

She eyed them with a grin. "I see. Well, follow me. I saved the best booth in the place for y'all."

They followed Rosie through the diner to a spacious booth at the back, where she placed laminated menus on the table. Lucas and Noah scrambled into the booth and eagerly picked up their menus, their eyes rounding with excitement.

Rob slid into the booth across from them.

"I'll give you a few minutes to decide," Rosie said. "How about drinks in the meantime?"

"Water, please," Lucas said.

Noah nodded in agreement.

Rob perused the menu and then put it down. "Boys, water

is fine, but it doesn't seem very special. How about a raspberry lemonade?"

"Oh, yeah!" Noah nodded eagerly.

"Thanks, Pastor Rob," Lucas said.

"You too?" Rosie asked, a brow arched.

"Absolutely," he replied.

When Rosie left, Noah looked at Rob. "Are we ordering special because of your birthday?"

"That's right."

"When did you say your birthday is, Pastor Rob?" Lucas asked.

"Soon." He picked the menu up again. "Now, let's find something special to eat."

The boys nodded, their eyes on the menu.

"What's that say?" Noah asked his big brother. He pointed to a spot on the menu.

"Tostaguac," Lucas said, slowly sounding out the word.

Noah's brows knit together and he grimaced. "*What is that?*"

Lucas shook his head, disgust on his face. "Doesn't matter. We want burgers and fries, right?"

"Right." Noah put down his menu. "Burger and French fries, please, Pastor Rob."

"You got it." Rob chuckled.

This was fun. He should have done it before and already regretted the omission. His self-exile hadn't benefitted anyone. What he needed was to keep stepping into the light. Stops at the bakery. More lunches with Lucas and Noah. This was definitely a wakeup call from the Lord to stop and smell the flowers. He fully intended to obey.

"That was the best lunch ever," Noah said an hour later as they headed to the artist's studio outside of town.

"Noah, you've said that like ten times already," Lucas said on a laugh.

"I can't help it," Noah replied. "It was yummy."

"No kidding," Rob said. "I can't remember the last time I had a burger that good." Not to mention the chocolate shake he'd splurged on. He'd have to run an extra mile tomorrow to burn off those calories.

"Maybe we can do it next year on your birthday, too," Noah said.

Rob chuckled. He was thinking the same thing. Would he be here next year? Another reason to hope so.

After a few minutes on the road, he glanced in the rear-view mirror at the boys in the back seat of his car, giggling as they pointed to views out the window. Rob smiled. They were fortunate to have each other. As an only child, he envied their relationship. Lucas didn't simply tolerate Noah. The affection between the brothers was obvious.

"Where are we going?" Lucas finally asked.

"There's an artist in town who makes stained-glass windows. I thought you might like to see how it works."

"Stained glass, like the church windows?" Noah asked.

"Exactly," Rob said.

"The church has a broken window," Noah said. "I saw it on Sunday."

"It sure does. Accidents happen." Rob glanced in his rear-view mirror and saw Lucas stare out the window, his jaw tense. There was a long silence, and Rob waited for Noah to say something about his brother. He didn't. Rob glanced at Lucas again. Soon the boy seemed to relax. So Hannah hadn't told her younger son about the window. Good for her.

Hannah was a good mother. A good person, period. He was only starting to understand the complexity of her character.

"This is it." Rob drove up a gravel drive to the parking area near a large red barn. To the left, a small white cottage sat in a shady thicket of trees and shrubbery. The pleasant melody of wind chimes could be heard through the open car window.

"I hear music," Noah chirped, "but I don't see any stained glass."

"You will," Rob said. He turned to face the boys in the back seat. "First, I have to tell you the rules. Listen to Miss Naomi's instructions. The studio has sharp pieces of glass and hot soldering tools. We all have to be very careful."

Both boys gave a somber nod.

"Let's go," Rob said.

All three of them stepped out of the car, and a tall, trim, mature woman in jeans and a denim shirt approached them from the barn's open doors. "Hello, hello!" she said. Her silver hair had been pulled back into a long ponytail that reached the middle of her back. She wore shiny brown cowboy boots with silver tips.

"You must be Miss Naomi," Rob said. He offered a hand. "I'm Pastor Rob Sterling and these young men are Lucas and Noah Bryant."

She took his hand firmly and nodded to the boys with a smile.

"I'm delighted to meet all of you. I'm finishing a small piece for one of my neighbors. It will replace her front door's glass. Would you like to see?"

Noah burst out with an enthusiastic "Yes," while Lucas offered a nervous nod.

"Come along, then, but don't touch anything. I'll show you my process."

They followed her into the barn studio until she stopped at a long table with a corkboard behind it. "I start with a paper design." Naomi pointed to the papers tacked to the board. "I know artists nowadays use computers, but I prefer plain old pencils and paper."

"What are those designs for?" Rob asked. He recognized one immediately but wanted to hear the artist explain it to the boys.

"Ah, well, that first small design is what I'm working on today—the hummingbird. I'll show that to you in a moment. The next one is more complex." She looked at the boys. "Does it look familiar?"

"That's the church window," Noah said. "Somebody busted it. Lester put a piece of wood over the window."

"Indeed. This is a church window." She smiled at Lucas. "Did you recognize the design?"

Lucas nodded, his face pale.

"I'll start on that project this week," Naomi said to Rob. "It's a little more complex with all the different colors in the design of the cross, but the result will be as spectacular as the old window, maybe more." Naomi waved a hand. "Come over to my other table."

Rob followed with Lucas dragging his feet behind them. This was a tough reality check for the boy, but a necessary one. It wasn't about guilt. Today was about understanding that there were real-world consequences for his actions.

The next table Naomi led them to was even larger, and on its surface, another paper design of the hummingbird project she mentioned had been laid out like a giant puzzle.

"This shows me where each piece of glass will go as it is created."

"It looks like a page from a coloring book," Rob said.

"That's correct," Naomi replied. "And this is the exact size of the hummingbird window. After I cut the glass shapes, I place them on the paper. Like a puzzle."

"What do you do next?" Rob asked.

Naomi pushed the pieces around on the paper, cocking her head as she assessed the design. "When I like what I see, it will be time to paint the glass."

Noah laughed. "You get to paint glass?"

"I do." Naomi smiled, obviously delighted at Noah's interest. "Then it goes into an oven to bake."

"Can I see the oven?" Noah asked.

"Of course." She led them to a large black box and raised the lid.

"It looks like the barbecue grill we have at home," Noah said.

"It does," Naomi said. "I have another that looks like a microwave oven."

"Cool," Noah murmured, his eyes wide.

"The last part is like tracing the outline of a picture in a coloring book. I outline all the pieces with lead. Next, I heat the lead. The lead is sort of like glue, connecting all the pieces of glass. There are a few more steps, but they're rather boring."

"Will you fit the stained glass into the church window yourself?" Rob asked.

"Oh, no." Naomi shook her head. "I don't do ladders and scaffolding anymore. My sons will come to the church, remove the old frame, and fit the new window."

Looking at the boys, she said, "Let's visit my shop store, out back. You can pick out a small stained-glass piece to take home and hang in your window. They all have a nice chain so that they can be displayed anywhere there's sunshine."

"Really?" Noah's eyes lit up.

"Yes. I have animals and birds. They reflect the light nicely when the sun shines."

"Pretty cool, huh?" Rob nudged Lucas as they followed behind to Naomi's store.

Lucas nodded. "I've been thinking. It's going to cost a lot of money for that window, isn't it?"

"Yes," Rob admitted. "But fortunately for you, sweat equity will cover the cost."

"What's sweat equity?"

"Working it off. Spring break is coming soon. Also, the rummage sale. I have a long list of things I need help with, and once the pantry is a reality, you can help there for a few hours a week."

Lucas nodded as he considered the answer. "I'll do whatever you need me to do, Pastor Rob. And thanks for not telling Noah."

"No need. You and I have a business arrangement. It doesn't involve anyone else except us and your mother." He smiled. "Now, go thank Miss Naomi for the tour and her generosity."

"Yes, sir." Lucas hurried to catch up with his brother.

Rob smiled as he followed close behind. They were good kids. He envied Hannah and admired her. She'd been through a rough time, yet she continued to see the positive at every turn. She set a good lesson for her sons.

And for Rob.

The grief and guilt in his heart at the loss of his wife remained. However, today reminded him that there was much to be said for an attitude like Hannah's. He was alive, and the Lord had a plan for his life. It was time to start seeing the gold among the rubble.

Hannah picked up her phone from the porch railing and settled against the cushions of the wicker chair. Almost 6:00 p.m. She'd checked every ten minutes since she got home. Except for the rare planned visits with their father or a trip to Hannah's mother every few weeks, the boys never went on outings without her.

An empty house was a novelty. She'd tidied the boys' rooms and started dinner before heading outside to tend to the horses. Then she wandered through the yard, unaccustomed to free time on her hands. Unaccustomed to the strange ache in her heart at her sons' absence. They were getting older, and Lucas especially was more and more involved with his friends.

It was true that she hadn't taken the time to cultivate outside activities or many close friends. Luna Perez was the only person she confided in. Maybe it was time to change that and get more involved. Tumbleweed was their home now. Developing roots in the community would be good for her and the boys.

Minutes later, the crunch of tires on gravel had Hannah looking up. She prayed that Lucas and Noah had been on their best behavior. Hopefully, Rob wouldn't regret today's invitation.

"Mom," Noah gushed as he raced up the porch steps to her side. "Look what we have."

He held up a blue bag, pulled out an object wrapped in tissue paper and soon held a beautiful stained-glass turtle on a chain. "From Miss Naomi. Luc has one, too. His is a dolphin."

"Wow, this is stunning." Her gaze scanned Noah's face, and she smiled, loving the joy in his expression.

"I guess you had fun."

"We had so much fun. I even played chess."

"Is that right?" She looked from Noah to Lucas, who climbed the steps behind his brother.

"I beat him," Lucas said, pride in his voice.

"Did you?" Hannah asked.

"Oh, yeah."

"Checkmate," Rob said, offering Lucas a high five. They both chuckled, while Noah, who'd lost, seemed thrilled just to be a part of the conversation.

Lucas carefully unwrapped the package in his hands and picked up the chain. A dolphin in shades of blue shimmered as it moved in the sunlight.

"Oh, Lucas, that's lovely. Miss Naomi is very generous to gift this to you." She smiled. "Did you see her projects?"

He nodded. "The window."

"Ah, yes, the window." She looked at Rob. "Thank you for taking them to such a special place."

"It was no problem. I enjoyed it as well."

Hannah glanced at her phone. "Time to wash up for dinner, boys. Thank Pastor Rob before you go."

"Thank you, Pastor Rob," they each echoed. The screen door slapped against the frame as Noah and Lucas jostled each other to get in the house first.

"Mom! You made cookies," Noah called out. "Can I have one?"

"May I," she corrected.

"May I have a cookie?" Noah called back.

"After dinner. You'll spoil your appetite." Hannah turned back to Rob, hesitant to ask the question she needed to. "How'd it go?"

"It really was a good day." He paused. "I'm sorry we're so late. I sort of lost track of time. After chess, we went to the park and tossed a softball around for a while. I figured you'd appreciate it if they burned off some energy."

Hannah stood and eyed Rob. His hair was tousled, and his ordinarily pristine dress shirt had a dark spot right smack dab in the middle of his chest. "You have something on your shirt."

Rob glanced down at the brown stain. His lips twitched.

"Busted. I may have spoiled their appetite already. After chess, we had ice cream."

"Before you played ball to burn off energy and sugar?" She laughed.

"Yeah." A sheepish expression crossed his face.

"Looks like chocolate to me."

"Correct." Rob smiled. "I've always been a messy ice cream eater. What can I say?"

Her breath caught when he released a chuckle. She'd never seen him so relaxed and, well…happy. The pain so often reflected in his green eyes was absent. His gaze met hers and held as he seemed to search her face for something.

In that fleeting moment, Hannah's heart swelled, taking her by surprise. She glanced away quickly. What was it about this man that left her confused and her heart thinking about things that she had put away in the cupboard long ago?

"Guess I better go," he said quietly.

"We'd be delighted if you join us for dinner. Chili and corn bread. Nothing fancy," she said. "Although you may be full after your late afternoon snack."

He released a low laugh. "I appreciate the invitation, but all this rummage sale and pantry planning has put me behind on my sermon. I've got some research to do."

"I understand." Hannah nodded. "Oh, and by the way, the ad for the rummage sale will be in Monday's paper. As we get closer, I'll reach out to our neighboring towns and get an ad in their papers, too, so folks put the date on their calendar and spend money in Tumbleweed. I'm sure the other weekly papers will agree to a little quid pro quo which will align with our low overhead goal."

"Great, and you'll do all that reaching out at your desk, not on your own time, right?"

"Yes. Boundaries. I'm keeping that in mind."

"Thank you."

She looked at him hesitantly, hoping that she wasn't about to overstep. "I had another idea. For the record, I had the idea at my desk."

Rob laughed. "Please share."

"How about if we charge a five-dollar entry to the event? Give folks wristbands good for both days. It will ensure that attendees take the event seriously and will bring in a little extra money. We're putting a temporary fence around the parking lot anyhow. We may as well utilize it and have someone man the entrance and take money. Maybe Ron Garcia."

"That's a genius idea, Hannah."

"Thank you." She smiled, pleased to have her idea so warmly received.

Rob gestured toward his car. "I should get out of your hair."

Hannah nodded. Yes, he should go, but for some reason, she longed for him to stay.

"Would you like some chili to take home with you? I made enough for an army. You can eat while you research."

A smile appeared at her offer. "Contrary to what you may have heard, I can cook. I don't get to as much as I'd like to with the generous deliveries by the ladies of Tumbleweed." He shrugged. "I don't want to offend anyone. It might surprise folks to know that, right now, I have a pot roast in the slow cooker waiting for my arrival."

"I'm impressed. Who taught you to cook?"

"My folks. They were school teachers most of my life. Then, about ten years ago, they gave up teaching to buy a diner. They're happy as can be, cooking up burgers and fries to the citizens of Humbolt."

"I love that they followed their dreams." Hannah frowned. "What's the Jim Stewart connection to your family? He mentioned he knows your folks."

"Dad and Jim were college roommates."

"Ah."

"Jim tracked me down last fall. I was working at a big church in Raleigh. A church so big it had five associate pastors. When he told me about Tumbleweed, I realized I was ready for a change."

Hannah nodded. "This is quite a change, then."

"Yeah. In a good way."

"Mom," Lucas called out. "The oven is beeping."

"Cornbread is ready," she murmured.

Rob nodded and stepped off the porch.

"Um, Pastor… I mean, Rob."

He turned back.

"Thank you. Today obviously meant a lot to the boys. To me, as well."

"I'm glad I could spend time with them. They're great kids and that makes you a great mom."

"Thank you."

"Have a good night, Hannah."

"You too, Rob. See you on Sunday." She smiled as he walked away.

The scent of chili greeted her as she entered the house and pulled the corn bread from the oven. She glanced around the kitchen and realized that the table was set. Noah and Lucas stood behind their chairs, smiling. She couldn't be prouder.

"What's this?" She feigned confusion. "I wonder who set the table."

Noah's grin widened. "We did."

"Thank you, both."

"Pastor Rob said you're working on a big project, and we should help more," Lucas added.

"He did, did he? Well, I appreciate your help." She smiled,

then filled their bowls with chili and placed a square of corn bread on their plates.

"Can I say prayers?" Lucas asked.

"You may." Hannah held their hands as they bowed their heads.

"Lord, thank You for this food and thank You for Pastor Rob. Amen."

"Amen," Hannah and Noah repeated.

"Mom, did you know Pastor Rob used to play sports in school?" Lucas asked.

"I did not." But she certainly could see it. He had the build of an athlete. Not that she ought to be noticing. However, some things were hard to ignore.

"He said we can toss the ball around again sometime," Lucas continued.

"Me, too," Noah said around a mouthful of food.

"Mouth closed when you chew, please," Hannah reminded him.

Her seven-year-old finished chewing, then swallowed. "Can we get a baseball mitt?"

"We can do that. Two mitts, coming up, next time we go to the city."

"Pastor Rob says I'd make a good pitcher because I have a strong arm," Lucas said.

Hannah buttered her corn bread and added a dollop of honey. "Did he?"

"Uh-huh."

Hannah nodded as they continued to chatter about their afternoon. Except for a few observations, she could barely get a word in. Their admiration for Rob Sterling had them talking nonstop.

"Do you want us to do the dishes?" Lucas asked her when they'd finished dinner.

"That's sweet of you to offer, but tonight you both get a night off. Go do your homework and get some reading in."

He quickly wiped his mouth with a napkin and raced out of the room with Noah. "Thanks, Mom."

"Yeah. Thanks, Mom," Noah repeated.

Hannah chuckled as she filled the sink with warm sudsy water.

Minutes later, footfalls echoed on the tile floor. She turned to see Lucas approaching.

"Mom?"

"Yes, Lucas." She dried her hands on a towel, sensing this was about to be a serious moment.

"Pastor Rob took us to see the lady who makes the windows for the church. Like the one I broke." He lowered his head for a moment and then met her gaze. Tears pooled in his eyes. "I'm real sorry I broke that window."

Hannah pulled him close. "I know you are, and I forgive you, and so does the Lord. We all mess up. That includes me. The important part is owning up to our mistakes, asking for forgiveness, and moving on." She smiled at him. "We're good, you and I. Got it?"

"Yes, ma'am." Lucas cocked his head and looked at her. "I like Pastor Rob. He's a regular guy."

"He is, isn't he?" she murmured.

When her son left the room, she stared out the window, thinking about the evening.

The boys had spent the last hour extolling the virtues of Pastor Rob. Luna was right. They needed a man in their lives. Both of them were starved for male attention. Their father had canceled their visits three months in a row, and there wasn't another male role model in their life. Even her little brother lived too far away to be of help.

It was indeed a blessing that Rob had offered to work

with Lucas. After one afternoon, she could already sense a change in him. Her eldest son seemed hopeful, and Rob had put that hope there.

It was all good, except September would be here soon enough, and Rob would likely be leaving. What would happen then? She couldn't bear the idea of her boy's heart being broken again.

Hannah swallowed hard, her gaze fixed on the sturdy oak, whose small greenish-yellow flowers had only started to come alive, as though the tree awoke from a long winter slumber.

She released a long sigh. Perhaps it wasn't only Lucas and Noah's hearts that she was concerned about.

Chapter Five

Rob's sneakers hit the pavement as he ran down Church Street where a huge banner advertising the rummage sale stretched across the street. Turning left at the corner, he kept his head down, counting silently, monitoring his pace while keeping an eye on the sidewalk where tree roots had caused the cement to buckle in places.

He'd started running four years ago when he'd been blind-sided by the loss of his wife. There wasn't a day that went by that he didn't run. Or think about the past and the future torn from him, though each day in Tumbleweed, the pain seemed a little less sharp and more like a constant ache that you learn to live with.

Lately, he'd come to understand that dwelling on yesterdays wouldn't do him or his parishioners any good. His optimistic secretary initiated that change in him, thanks to the example she provided. Change had cracked open a door in his life, though walking through would be on his terms—when he was worthy.

"Let us run with patience the race that is set before us," Rob murmured as he ran, quoting Hebrews 12:1.

The Lord had laid out the course before him. By coming to Tumbleweed, Rob continued to trust that the destination, though unknown, would be precisely the right one.

One. Strike. Two. Strike. Rob counted his footfalls as he ran.

Overhead, a bird chirped in a maple tree. Rob didn't listen to music so he could hear nature and appreciate being alive.

Sweat trickled down his back, and he tugged on the neck of his T-shirt to wipe his face. He still wasn't used to the humidity in Texas. It was only the second week of March and it was sixty percent humidity. Good for the spring flowers but not for him.

Turning again onto Main Street, the aroma of fresh coffee from the bakery hit him, luring him closer and closer. Usually, he ignored the siren's call, heading home to shower and dress for work. Having the parsonage on Church Street, steps from the church, was handy.

Maybe he'd change up his routine today and grab a coffee and a croissant before he went home to clean up.

He pulled to a sudden stop outside the bakery at the sight of a sign in the window. The neon pink sign advertised the first annual Tumbleweed Community Rummage Sale, sponsored by the Tumbleweed Church, Big W Ranch, and Stewart Properties, to benefit the Tumbleweed Community Church Pantry. The sign was only a glimpse of what he'd heard Mayor Louise and her team had done in the last week since the board meeting. Donations were arriving at an almost alarming rate. The storage room was already full.

"Morning, Pastor."

Rob turned from the window and smiled at a pleasant, older woman entering the bakery. "Morning."

Eight a.m. on a Saturday, and the bakery had a steady flow of patrons in and out the door. Rob had heard that Sweet Dream Bakery's cinnamon rolls were legendary.

"Morning, Pastor," someone else said from behind him. A tall gentleman offered a tip of his straw Stetson.

"Good morning." Rob tried to place the man but couldn't.

Focus, he reminded himself. Get out of your head. This is your flock. They deserve more.

Rob entered the shop and paused momentarily, taking in the pink-and-black decor and the aroma of coffee, cinnamon, vanilla and fresh bread. Every table was occupied, and the entire place hummed with happy patrons.

He approached the counter, where Luna Perez assisted another customer. Though he hadn't been in the shop before, he'd interacted with the spunky baker when she'd generously donated pastries to the church for various events.

"Hannah," Luna called over her shoulder. "Got a minute to help out here?"

"I'm not in a rush," Rob said. "Happy to wait my turn."

"This is the first time you've been in my bakery," Luna said with a smile. "Of course, I'm going to give you the VIP treatment, Pastor."

"My apologies for not stopping by sooner. I recently had one of your chocolate cupcakes and wow." Rob offered a chef's kiss.

Luna smiled, pleased at the compliment. "Thank you." She glanced behind him and chuckled. "However, it's even better to have you here in person. You're good for business."

"I am?"

"Yes, sir, Pastor Rob, you are." Luna nodded toward the shop's window as she filled a box with plump blueberry muffins for the customer standing in front of him.

Rob looked behind him in time to see two middle-aged women on the sidewalk peering into the bakery. They gave him an enthusiastic wave. Surprised and a bit confused, he offered a quick wave in return.

"Pastor Rob." Hannah's voice had him turning back to the counter. "May I interest you in a cinnamon roll? They're on sale until noon. Two for the price of one. Today's flavors are maple cinnamon, salted caramel, and frosted pecan."

Rob smiled at the dab of flour on her chin. He automatically raised a hand to brush it away, then quickly stopped, stunned at his behavior.

What was he thinking?

He and Hannah were friends. That was all. He still wasn't sure what to make of the incident yesterday when their gazes connected, and his heart sped up. The whole thing had confused him. Still did. Maybe he should cut back on his caffeine.

"Pastor?" She paused. "Are you all right?"

"Yes. Sorry. Lots on my mind." Rob cleared his throat. "Those cinnamon rolls sound amazing, but you know I'm a chocolate fan. I'll take a large coffee to go and a chocolate croissant, please."

"Yes, sir." Her lips twitched as she said the word *sir*.

While Hannah poured his coffee into a to-go cup, he placed a bill on the counter. Luna reached over and handed it back to him. "On the house today. I told you, you're good for business. Come by more often."

"I certainly will," he replied.

Hannah slid his coffee and a pastry bag across the counter. She leaned forward. "See the four fellas in the corner playing checkers?"

Rob glanced around until he saw the foursome. "I do."

"The gentleman with round glasses, wearing the navy-blue military ball cap with gold lettering, is Abner Goldby."

"One hundred years young, World War II navy veteran Abner Goldby?"

"That's the one. His son drops him off here every Saturday for a few hours and then picks him up again."

"Thanks, Hannah. I appreciate it." This was an opportunity to start doing right by his congregation. Letting them know he saw each and every person.

He headed over to the group and stopped at their table. The men, all wearing various ball caps representing their military service branch, began to stand. Rob held up a hand. "No need to stand. I'm the one who should be standing. Thank you for your service, gentlemen."

"Good morning, Pastor Sterling," Abner said. He squinted up at Rob.

"Sir, it's an honor to have you as a parishioner of Tumbleweed Community Church." Rob offered his free hand.

The man's eyes lit up, the wrinkles appearing as his smile reached from one side of his face to the other. "Why, thank you." He shook Rob's hand, straightening in his seat. "And you should know how much I enjoy your sermons."

As Abner introduced his friends, Rob shook their hands, committing their names to memory.

"It's a pleasure to meet you, gentlemen," Rob said. "If you'll excuse me, I've got to get to work on my sermon. The Boss is watching." He pointed skyward.

The men chuckled at his words.

"I look forward to Sundays, Pastor Sterling," Abner said. "You always give me something to think about. Glad to have you here in Tumbleweed."

"Thank you, I'm honored to be here." Honored and humbled to be acknowledged by veterans who served their country. The exchange had unexpectantly touched Rob down to his core.

Leaving the bakery, he held the door for the two women on the sidewalk who had decided to come in. "Ladies, good morning."

"Oh, Pastor Sterling, good morning. I don't think I've ever noticed you in the bakery before," one of the women said.

"You haven't," he said with a grin. "But I intend to rectify that by visiting again next Saturday. Maybe I'll see you."

Both women giggled. "Absolutely."

He turned and caught Hannah's eye and winked. She was a smart lady, that Hannah.

Rob stepped out onto the sidewalk and turned toward the empty building next door. He studied the shop through the front glass. A sense of pride he hadn't felt since he'd moved to Tumbleweed overtook him.

Tumbleweed Community Church Pantry.

"This is ours, Lord," he said aloud, not caring who heard him.

It didn't matter that the odds were stacked against the venture. Rob knew in his heart the pantry was going to happen. He smiled as he crossed the street, his steps light, his heart full.

"Hannah, there's an accordion and a penny-farthing in the choir room." The music director, Henry Mattigan, stood in the church kitchen doorway. He adjusted his plaid bow tie and frowned as though completely baffled.

Hannah examined the contents of her lunch bag one more time before looking up. "What's a penny-farthing?"

"Oh, you know. That high wheeler that looks like it stepped out of the nineteenth century."

"Oh, that. Okay, but what about the other? I don't suppose you could find a use for an accordion?"

Henry ran a hand over his bald head. "Tomorrow evening, thirty children will arrive to practice the cantata for Easter service, including your youngest. Not a one of them can play the accordion."

"Well, that's unfortunate." She unwrapped her sandwich and realized that somehow she'd managed to mix up Noah's lunch with her own. Today her son would dine on meatloaf with provolone, her favorite, while she had a peanut butter-and-jelly sandwich. Noah would not be happy.

She was not a fan of peanut butter and jelly. Hannah sighed and looked up at the music director.

"The storage room is already full, Henry. The rummage sale will be over in ten days."

"I understand that we all have to do our part, but I expected boxes, not piles of…stuff," he said.

"Let me finish lunch and I'll replace the accordion and the bike with boxes. We have lots of those."

"I appreciate that, Hannah." He turned away.

"Thank you," she said. "But…"

Henry stopped walking and turned back. "But?"

"Donations are still pouring in like manna from heaven. Nonstop, for a week now, Henry. I'm thrilled everyone is excited to participate, but if things don't slow down we'll definitely have to put other items besides boxes in the choir room."

She met Henry's gaze to be sure he understood. "It's inevitable that at some point you'll have to hold practice in the chancel."

"Today is merely a reprieve?"

"Correct. Oh, and Henry, don't forget about the little birthday celebration in the kitchen. Forty minutes."

"I won't." Henry smiled as though thoroughly tickled. "Such a lovely gesture, Hannah."

"Pastor Rob is far from home. The least we can do is celebrate his birthday. Just remember, it's a secret."

Hannah took a bite of her sandwich and grimaced as her tongue stuck to the roof of her mouth. Peanut butter. Not only did she have the wrong lunch, but she had left home wearing one black shoe and one blue shoe. She glanced down at her feet and cringed.

Monday was her day off, but she'd spent the day fielding calls on her personal phone from parishioners about the rummage sale. So much for work-life boundaries. The line in the sand was gone.

Today wasn't much different. Nonstop phone calls since she walked in the door. Why, she hadn't even gotten to lunch until now. And forget her regular duties. They'd fallen to the wayside.

It hadn't escaped her that the quote on the kitchen bulletin board was laughing at her.

Life is all about finding calm in the chaos.
—Anonymous.

She hadn't found it yet. Hannah checked the lunch bag. No cookies either. Instead, there were carrot sticks. Noah's teacher would surely send home a note reminding her about the effects of sugar on young minds and the teacher's patience.

That was supposed to be her excess sugar. She bit into a carrot stick. Those cookies would have been tasty about now.

Using the teeny tiny straw that came with the juice box, also in Noah's lunch, Hannah sucked up the last drops with an unsatisfying slurp. She shoved carrot sticks back into the lunch sack and dropped the bag onto her desk as she headed to the choir room.

Henry was right. The room was much too small for anything but boxes. The high-wheel bicycle seemed to have grown since she'd instructed Lester to put it in the room early this morning.

A penny-farthing. Interesting name. Where had it come from? A circus? And what was it doing in Tumbleweed?

After struggling to grip the handlebars, Hannah carefully wheeled it around stacks of chairs, half a dozen music stands, and into the hallway. Then the oversized front tire slammed into the wall before bouncing sideways, nearly knocking her to the ground. She wrestled with the cast-iron frame, attempting to turn the bike in the other direction.

"Hannah, what are you doing?" Rob asked as he strode down the hall. "And where did this bike come from?"

"Moving a penny-farthing. Isn't it obvious?" She kept her eyes on the bike and not on Rob.

He started laughing. "Sure. Totally obvious. How can I help?"

When he reached out to guide the bike by the frame, his hand covered hers. Stunned by the contact, Hannah slid her fingers away.

"I've got this." She nodded toward the open doorway behind her. "You could grab the accordion from the choir room."

"Grab the accordion. I can do that. Where am I taking the accordion?"

"Both will go in Sam's office. Our beloved associate pastor is only here on Wednesday and Sunday. I doubt he'll even notice tomorrow."

Rob laughed again. "Oh, he'll notice. But look on the bright side. Today is Tuesday, so we've got time to come up with a plan B."

By the time she'd arranged the bike against the wall behind Sam's desk, Rob came in with the accordion. He glanced around the tiny office, finally placing the instrument on a chair.

"What's next?" he asked.

"Boxes," Hannah said. "Boxes from the storage room need to go into the choir room."

"Is there a reason for playing musical box donations?" Arms crossed, Rob eyed her.

"I'm hoping it will create some calm in the chaos."

"I'm glad you have dreams." He laughed and followed her down the hall.

Halfway to the storage room, Rob stopped and frowned, confused, as he looked around. "Do you smell chocolate?"

Hannah grimaced at his words but kept moving, feigning ignorance.

There was a two-layer dark chocolate truffle cake covered with milk chocolate buttercream on the other side of the building, safely tucked away in the bridal dressing room. Could he really sniff it out from here?

She inhaled deeply and shook her head. "All I smell is disinfectant and lemon polish. Lester washes and buffs the floor on Tuesdays."

"I didn't even see him this morning."

"Spring is his busy season. Did you know Lester has his own landscaping business? He's in and out of the church as fast as he can this time of year."

"I wasn't aware."

Hannah raised her brows.

"Mea culpa." Rob lifted a palm in defense. "Lester's business is now committed to memory."

They began to enter the storage room at the same time, nearly colliding with each other. Hannah jumped back while Rob waved a hand, ushering her ahead.

"After you," he said.

She stepped into the room, glanced around and blew out a loud breath. The stack of boxes and other items seemed to grow exponentially by the hours.

It was a very good thing that she wore jeans to work today. She'd done nothing but shlep boxes and trash bags filled with donations to this room since 8:00 a.m. There had even been a pile of items dropped off when the church was closed waiting for her outside the building when she arrived this morning. The rummage sale was off to a great start.

Rob's gaze spanned the room, taking in the tall stacks of boxes. "I'll have to send Dixie flowers. The *Gazette* sure got the word out. But do we have a plan for after the rummage sale ends?" Rob asked. He picked up two large boxes with ease.

Hannah grabbed a banker box and then put a smaller box on top. "A plan for what?"

"For what will happen to items that don't sell."

"I'll call the Tumbleweed Thrift Store. I'm sure they'll help us out."

"What if the remains are more than they can handle?" He eyed the mountain of donations. "What if there's furniture left over? The thrift store isn't very big."

"We can find a donation place in Beaumont or Houston. Some place with a truck to haul it all away." Hannah shrugged. "That is the least of our problems."

"What is the 'most' of our problems?" Rob asked.

"I don't believe in superstition," Hannah said, "but I'd still rather not say aloud. A positive mindset is in our best interest." She moved out the door. There was no way she would mention that the weather report had hinted at a possibility of rain. Nope. Instead, she'd commit the issue to prayer.

"Ever consider a career in crisis management?" Rob called from behind her.

Hannah offered a humorless laugh. "My entire life has been crisis management."

They entered the choir room and added their boxes to the stack against the far wall.

Henry popped his head into the room from his office and smiled. "Thank you both." He glanced at his watch and shot Hannah a meaningful look.

She nodded.

"All righty," Henry said. "I think I'll go make a fresh pot of coffee."

"What was that look he gave you all about?" Rob asked when the music director left.

"What look?" Hannah countered. Dodging Rob's questions was becoming more challenging. The man was sharp and would figure out something was going on any minute now.

The sound of the employee entrance door of the church building slamming shut had both Hannah and Rob stepping into the hall.

"Beat you to the kitchen," Noah yelled.

"Shh," Lucas said to his brother. "Mom said we have to be quiet when we come into the Lord's house."

"I'm not talking loud. You are," Noah retorted.

"School's out," Hannah singsonged, relieved to avoid Rob's question.

"Are we gonna get cake now?" Noah asked.

"Boys, we can hear you," Hannah called, hoping to silence them.

"Oops," Noah whispered as he rounded the corner and faced his mother and Rob.

"Let's go to the kitchen," Hannah said. "How was your meatloaf sandwich, Noah?"

Noah gagged. "I ate the cookies. They were really good."

"You don't like meatloaf?" Rob asked. He followed them to the kitchen and pulled down his coffee mug.

"No way," Noah said.

Henry turned from the sink, anticipation in his eyes. "Are we ready?"

"Not yet," Hannah said.

"Ready for what?" Rob asked.

"Cantata practice," Henry improvised. He started a conversation about the children's choir with Rob. To his credit, though he appeared confused, Rob didn't say a word.

Hannah whispered to Lucas. "Go to the bridal dressing room and get the cake and ice cream from the refrigerator, please. Mr. Mattigan will be along to help you."

"Me, too?" Noah asked.

"No, you've helped enough. Stay right here." She coughed loudly. "Henry, Lucas needs your assistance."

"I'm on it." The music director dashed out of the room, leaving Rob staring after him.

"Didn't think I'd make it in time." Lester, the custodian, a stocky man in his forties, burst into the room with a bandanna around his head and a trowel in the back pocket of his jeans. He headed to the sink, turned on the water, and washed his hands, sluicing water on his face.

"In time for what?" Rob asked.

"He's going to take a look at that magnolia outside my office window." Hannah prayed she wouldn't be struck down for fibbing.

"Ah," Rob nodded. "How's the landscaping business, Lester?"

"Busy as can be, Pastor. And that is a very good thing." Lester wiped his wet face with a paper towel. "Thanks for asking."

Rob winked at Hannah, clearly pleased with himself.

"Hey, there." Patty Wright strolled into the kitchen and set two shopping bags on the table. "Look who I found in the parking lot."

Mayor Louise and Dixie Jarrett followed Patty into the room.

"Did we have a board meeting I forgot about?" Panic washed over Rob's face as Jim Stewart and Rob Garcia also entered the kitchen.

"We got it, Mom," Lucas said. He hauled a large tub of chocolate vanilla swirl ice cream to the table. Right behind him, was Henry with the sheet cake.

"Look at that cake," Dixie said. "Luna has outdone herself."

"Aha! I thought I smelled chocolate." Rob grinned, his gaze on Hannah.

"Happy Birthday, Pastor Rob," Lucas said.

"What?" Rob looked at everyone. "I…well… Wow. This is a surprise. Thank you."

"Oh, it was all Lucas and Noah," Hannah said. "They let me know about your birthday."

Patty pulled paper plates and plastic utensils out of one bag, and a wrapped present out of the other. She handed the gift to Rob. "Happy Birthday, Pastor Rob. This is from all of us."

"I… I don't know what to say."

"Nothing to say," Jim Stewart replied. "Open it up. I want to see what we bought you."

Rob laughed awkwardly and turned his attention to the gift. He carefully opened the box and removed the lid, before parting the white tissue paper. Inside was a heather-gray T-shirt.

"A running shirt," Rob said. "I love it. Thank you."

"Hold it up," Louise said. Excitement laced her voice.

Dixie positioned her phone to snap a picture. "Smile. This is for the *Gazette*."

Rob held up the shirt so the words on the back were visible and read them aloud. "I never dreamed I'd be a 'super cool pastor,' but here I am, killing it."

"You surely are, Pastor Rob," Ron Garcia said. The adults in the room laughed.

Louise grabbed a box of candles and turned to Rob. "How old did you say you are?"

"Old enough to know better than to answer that question," Rob said with a chuckle. "You better just put a couple on there, or else we'll set off the smoke detector."

She put two candles on the cake and lit them before nodding to Henry. "Do you want to lead us in song?"

Rob grinned, his face reddening as his friends offered a rousing rendition of "Happy Birthday" followed by applause. Despite his unease at being the center of attention, Rob's eyes said he was happy. Really happy. Hannah's heart melted at the sight that made this chaotic day worthwhile.

When she handed him a generous slice of cake on a paper plate, Rob inspected the swirls of thick chocolate buttercream, topped with cocoa dusted truffles. "Whoa. This is some cake."

"That spectacular cake is your birthday present from Luna. She couldn't be here."

"That Luna is pretty special."

"She is," Hannah agreed. It was Luna who encouraged Hannah to follow through with this impromptu party.

As the group chatted and enjoyed their cake and ice cream, Hannah leaned against the counter, pleased. Everyone had managed to stop by, though they surely had places to be. They all liked and respected Rob. Though he claimed he hadn't been at the top of his game these past months, she knew that he had underestimated his impact on the town.

After an hour or so, the guests slowly left, giving Rob final birthday greetings.

"You've got quite a bit of cake to take home," Hannah said as she began to clean up.

"Let's leave it in the fridge here for everyone to enjoy," Rob replied. The grin on his face hadn't eased in the last hour.

"That's very generous of you." She wiped down the table

with a cloth and tucked in the chairs. "Boys, grab your stuff. I'll meet you outside."

She followed Rob down the hall, where she flipped off the lights in her office. "Do you want me to help you check the building?"

"No, I've got it. You've done enough."

"Well, Happy Birthday. Thanks for letting us share your special day." She smiled. "Although I don't actually know which day it is. The boys were certain it was this week." She shrugged. "Most people celebrate all month long these days."

"Um, Hannah…" Rob hesitated. He adjusted his glasses and took a deep breath. "About that."

"About what?"

"My birthday."

She released a small gasp. "Oh, no. Did I embarrass you? As usual, I just steamrolled ahead. I forget that there are people in the world who don't like to have their business out there." She paused. "I mean, I know you're used to public attention, but this is personal, isn't it?"

"Actually, I'm truly touched by what you did." He glanced around, his gaze finally returning to her. "I'm feeling a bit dishonest at the moment. All the trouble you and everyone went to."

"You deserve it. Everyone was on board when I mentioned the idea."

"But…"

She eyed him, confused. "What is it?"

"My birthday isn't until June."

Hannah blinked. "The boys said it was coming up soon. Lucas was certain that it was this month." She paused. "'Any day now,' he said."

"June is soon. As opposed to December." He nodded solemnly. "I take full responsibility. I told them my birthday was soon as an excuse to go to the Friendly Fork for lunch. They told me it was only for special occasions."

She stared at him for a moment. Then she started laughing, unable to stop. Near to tears, she finally caught her breath. "Oh, my. And you played along with all of this?"

"Once I saw the cake," he said with a laugh. "I was afraid you'd take it away. I mean, what a cake."

"Yes. What a cake is right." Hannah smiled for a moment. Then reality hit. "Are we going to tell anyone about this?"

"Eventually." He glanced at her, his expression hopeful. "For now, can it be our little secret?"

"Our little secret," Hannah repeated. She liked the sound of that.

Chapter Six

Hannah was certain that today would go on record as the busiest Thursday ever. The phone hadn't stopped ringing. Though it was a little after the noon hour, she hadn't managed to get far from her desk. She blamed it on the rummage sale, because if this was the new normal at the church, she would have to petition for a part-time receptionist.

When the phone rang yet again, she glared at it darkly, stabbed the speaker button with the end of her pencil and answered with a perkiness she was far from feeling. "Tumbleweed Community Church. This is Hannah. How may I assist you?"

"Hi, Hannah. This is Tom Archer trying to reach Rob Sterling again."

The word *again* hung in the silence between them, a clear signal that Rob had not called him back. She couldn't help but wonder why.

"Hello, Mr. Archer. I'll send you to his voicemail."

"No, no, wait. Is Rob in?"

"I'm sorry. Pastor Rob is in back-to-back meetings all morning."

"Okay." Tom Archer gave a resigned sigh. "Voicemail it is. Thank you, Hannah."

Hannah continued working on a reminder email to the local newspapers. She hoped they would make good on their promise to share information about the upcoming Tumbleweed rummage sale in their editions next week. A quick glance at the calendar on her desk reminded her that there were a mere eight days until the big event.

On the other side of the desk was a folder labeled Tumbleweed Church Community Pantry in big letters. She grabbed the folder and opened it, checking off items on her to-do list. Rob had instructed her to proceed with prepping the pantry for opening day, scheduled for the Monday after Easter.

Three weeks ago, Hannah said she had peace about the pantry. She had no idea how the Lord would pull it off, but, now, after seeing the community participation that overflowed the storage room, the supply room, and half the choir room, she realized He had a plan, that exceeded expectations.

Once again, the phone rang, and Hannah hit the speaker while eyeing the paint samples in the folder. "Tumbleweed Community Church. Good morning. This is Hannah. How may I assist you?"

"Morning, Hannah, this is Louise Mitchell," the mayor chirped. "I'm going to need someone to head over to my neighbor's place today. Her daughter called me. She just moved her mama into a retirement facility and they'd love nothing more than to donate items to the church."

"Donate what, Louise?"

"Kitchen items, mostly. Dishes, pots, and pans, along with some collectibles. Everything is boxed up and ready to go, but the catch is, they need it gone today."

"Today?" Hannah grimaced as she grabbed a fresh legal pad from her desk drawer. "Can you give me an address?"

"Sure. I should warn you, though. The house is off the beaten path. Your vehicle GPS navigation won't help." Louise rattled off directions.

"Left at the big red barn and then right at the silo?" Hannah repeated.

"That's right."

"Okay, I've got it."

"Are you going to be able to get out there today?"

A tap at Hannah's door had her turning her head to see Rob standing in the doorway. "Louise, I'm going to put you on hold for a minute while I check on something."

"Surely. No problem."

"I can drive the van out there," Rob said.

"What about your last meeting?" Hannah asked.

"I just got an email canceling."

She nodded and pressed the speaker button again. "It's all taken care of, Louise. Pastor Rob is happy to take the church van out there."

"Y'all are wonderful," Louise said. "I'm so excited about this rummage sale. I can hardly wait until next week. The Tumbleweed Ladies' Auxiliary met after service Wednesday evening, and we're going to wear matching vests during the sale and assist customers. Kind of like greeters at those big box stores, but ours will be pink. Dixie and I are sewing up the vests this weekend."

"Oh, Louise, that is a terrific idea."

"Thanks, Hannah. Talk to you soon."

After Hannah hung up the phone, she looked at Rob. "I'm going with you. I could use a break. Besides, there are a lot of boxes, according to Louise."

She paused and glanced at her watch, calculating the drive out and back. The boys would be out of school before they returned.

"Ask Luna to watch the boys," Rob said as though reading her mind.

"Oh, I hate to bother her."

"I thought she was your friend."

"She is. But she's already doing so much. She's designing the web page for the pantry, for one. And are you aware that fifty percent of her sales during the rummage sale are going to the pantry?"

"That's very generous of her but it has nothing to do with watching Noah and Lucas." He met her gaze. "Ask her, Hannah. If she says no, we'll find another solution."

He was right, though she hadn't missed the we part. She could get used to being part of a team. A team with Rob Sterling. Hannah picked up her cell phone and made the call.

Minutes later, they were in the church van, on their way to pick up the donations.

"Louise wasn't kidding when she said this was off the beaten path," Rob said.

"Beaten is a good descriptor," Hannah said. She put a hand on the dashboard when they hit another pothole, jostling the entire vehicle. She felt like a bronc rider working to stay in the saddle.

"Sorry. I'm trying to avoid them. The problem is there are more potholes than road. The cattle grates don't help, either." He shook his head. "The shocks on this van are non-existent. I pity the parishioner seated in the back." Rob looked at her. "And the front passenger seat."

"I'll live. After the third pothole I realized that I've been out here a time or two. As I recall, there's a fresh fruit stand down the road where they sell jams and jellies in the offseason."

"Maybe we can check it out on the way back."

The van slowed down and Hannah's gaze darted to Rob. "Everything okay? We aren't out of gas, are we?"

"No. Look at that field." Rob pulled over to the side of the road and rolled down his window.

"Pretty, isn't it?" Her gaze skipped over the waves of purple-hued flowers and lush green foliage in an endless grassy meadow. Overhead, the day had delivered a sky as blue and pretty as a robin's egg, framing the view that stretched to the horizon.

"I've never seen anything like it before." He undid his seat belt and opened his door. "I think this is my sign to stop and smell the flowers."

"Smell the flowers?"

"Yeah. It's a little inside joke between me and the Lord."

Pushing the buckle on her seat belt, Hannah worked to unlock the device. "Wait. My seat belt is stuck."

"That's not good." Rob leaned back into the van and examined the buckle from the driver's side. "Something isn't right with the tongue and latch."

When Rob raised his head, Hannah realized he was mere inches away. She sat transfixed, unable to move as her heart beat and beat and beat. Surely he could hear it. Hannah swallowed as she realized that Rob, too, seemed frozen, his gaze dragging slowly from her eyes to her mouth. There was something different in his expression, something that made her long to lean closer.

Then he cleared his throat and stepped back, reaching into his jeans and pulling out a pocketknife. With a poke at the buckle using the blade, it disengaged.

He tucked the knife away without looking at her, adjusted his glasses, and turned away. "We'll need to get that checked. There must be some sand or dirt in the latch. Probably only gets stuck every once in a while."

"Yes," she murmured, catching her breath and willing her heart to stop pounding. They would definitely need to check that out.

"Come on," he said with a nod to the meadow. "I have to

get some pictures of this to send my folks. This is unbelievable."

Hannah walked around the van to follow Rob into the field.

"We love our wildflowers in Texas," Hannah said softly. She'd overanalyze what just happened between them later. Much later. "Take care not to step on the flowers, or they won't seed and bloom again next year."

"What kind of flowers are they?" Rob asked.

"Bluebonnets, of course."

"What do you mean, of course? I don't see any blue flowers out there."

"They're still bluebonnets, and they're the state flower. All six varieties are the state flower." She laughed.

"What's that over there?" He aimed his phone camera at a pocket of red.

"Indian paintbrush."

"I've never seen anything so vibrant," Rob said.

"All of this…" Hannah waved her hand around. "This is just the preshow. Come April and May, the wildflowers really take off. Photographers come from all over the world to take photos."

Rob turned and snapped a picture of her.

"Hey, keep that on the flowers." She held up a hand to block her face. "I'm not photogenic."

"I'll be the judge of that." He angled his phone for another shot. "You were saying that you're a Texas wildflower expert."

Hannah picked a small purple bloom and inhaled the floral and grape scent. "I'm a third-generation Texan. That's considered a newcomer. But I've seen quite a few springs."

"Third generation. Your great-grandparents started things?"

"Yes. My maternal great-grandmother came here with my

great-grandfather, another Okie, and they bought a dairy farm near Beaumont, though they didn't know a thing about farming."

"The pioneer spirit," Rob observed.

"Apparently. They had twin boys, and my grandparents had one child. My mother."

"What about your father?"

She shrugged and looked away. "Oh, he's from around here. Beaumont. The Southeast Texas area. My father is a wanderer. Took off when I was ten, and my brother was five."

"I'm sorry to hear that."

"Me, too. My mother did a great job raising us alone, but she went back into the job market when he took off with few marketable skills of her own. Those were tough times."

Hannah paused, reigning in the unpleasant memories. Talking about her father always knotted her up and she generally avoided the topic.

So why was she sharing now?

She cleared her throat and worked to relax. "I've learned a lot from her, and it has served me well. The biggest lesson was to stay one step ahead of trouble because it always arrives when you least expect it."

"Meaning you always expect the other shoe to drop?"

She blinked at his words so casually delivered. "What? No. Not at all."

Rob looked at her. "That's what you just said. And here I took you for an optimist."

"I *am* an optimist." Hannah dropped the flowers, suddenly annoyed. "An optimist who's always prepared."

"For the other shoe to drop."

Hannah jerked back. Her gaze skittered over him, but he continued to snap pictures. No. He was wrong. She was the most positive person there was. He could ask anyone.

When silence stretched out between them, he turned to look at her and frowned as though confused by her reaction. "There's nothing wrong with your point of view," Rob said. "Understandable as well." He gestured toward the van. "Ready?"

"Yes." The response came out stiffly.

They drove for a few miles in silence as Hannah mulled Rob's words. She was overthinking. Wasn't she? Either way, Rob was wrong. His assessment completely off base.

"There's the red barn," Rob said. He turned left per the mayor's instructions and then turned right at the silo. Eventually a mailbox came into view with the address they were looking for.

"Yes. That's it," Hannah said. "Turn into that drive."

Rob pulled into a long gravel drive that led to a regal two-story brick colonial home with a detached garage. Perfectly manicured bushes surrounded the house and a large magnolia with white blooms sat in the middle of the front lawn. The yard, with its recently mowed lawn, crisply edged, held a For Sale sign.

Most of the homes in the vicinity were farmhouses and manufactured homes.

A red brick walkway led to a covered portico with four regal off-white balustrades. At least two dozen boxes were stacked in front of a burgundy double front door.

"A beautiful house, isn't it?" Hannah asked.

Rob scratched his head. "Yeah. Do folks usually build mansions like this in the middle of nowhere? I'm not sure I understand the rationale."

She chuckled. "This is Texas. You don't need rationale."

Hannah pressed on the buckle of the seat belt, praying it would work. It did. She jumped out of the van and assessed the front walk.

"I'm glad we brought handcarts," Rob said as he pulled open the back doors of the van.

"And I'm glad there's no furniture."

A cool breeze accompanied them as they loaded the van. Thirty minutes later, the vehicle was full and they were on the road again.

They had just passed the wildflower field, where they'd stopped on the way to the house, when a low-to-the-ground animal ambled into the road. Hannah braced herself, preparing for a collision.

Rob must have seen it as well. He jerked the wheel to the left, diverting them off the road toward a slight embankment, which boasted yet another pothole. The van shifted with a loud, scraping clunk.

Hannah took her hand from the dash and looked at Rob. "That was close."

"What sort of animal was that?" he asked.

"Armadillo."

"You're kidding, right?"

"No. Armadillos are known for wandering across the road this time of year. They can do a lot of damage to a vehicle. We probably scared him. I appreciate you not making him roadkill."

"You're welcome. Keep that appreciation in mind once I assess the damage to the van."

Rob got out of the car, walked to the front of the vehicle, and knelt to look under the bumper.

Hannah groaned when she realized that the seat belt was stuck again. She pulled a pen from her tote bag and poked at the buckle, finally freeing herself.

"What's the verdict?" She walked to the front of the van. The tires weren't flat, but one was pointed straight, the other to the left. The entire van sat slightly lopsided due to the pothole.

"Tie rod," Rob said. He stood and dusted the dry, red dirt from his knees. "We aren't going anywhere."

"Can we fix it?"

"Nope. I don't even know how a tow is going to get that thing on a flatbed like that."

"I guess we'll find out. I've got the number of the local repair shop on my phone. My ancient Chevy has been towed a few times." Hannah called and explained the situation to the repair shop. Then she turned to Rob, who leaned against the van, arms crossed.

"An hour minimum," she said.

"Now I'm sorry I skipped lunch." Rob shook his head. "That cake in the fridge would be good about now, along with a hot cup of coffee." He smacked his lips. "What did you call it? Buttercream truffle?"

"Yes, chocolate buttercream truffle." She walked to the passenger side and pulled out her tote bag. "I brought a sandwich and added a couple of granola bars and two waters." She laughed. "You know, just in case."

Rob chuckled. "There's a bit of irony in this situation. I'm in the middle of nowhere with an optimist I accused of always being prepared for disaster. My timing needs work."

"We can discuss your mischaracterization of my character, later," Hannah said. "Right now, I'm starving, too." She dug in the bag, pulled out the sandwich and offered him half. "Here you go."

"Thank you." He shook his head as he unwrapped the sandwich. "In the future, remind me to keep my insights to myself. I should know better after spending time with Lucas. 'Think before you move' is a basic endgame chess strategy." He shrugged. "I'm rambling. What I should be doing is apologizing. I'm sorry for opening my big mouth, Hannah."

"Apology accepted." She sighed and met his gaze. "Maybe

I'm overreacting a bit. I want badly to get things right. I probably ought to ease up."

"You're the most 'get things right' person I know."

Hannah searched his gaze and realized he meant it. "Thank you."

His words warmed her, while at the same time she couldn't help but wonder about the truth of his original assessment.

Was she waiting for the other shoe to drop instead of trusting the Lord completely? Rob had certainly given her something to pray about.

"How long did the repair place say it was gonna take to get here?" Rob asked. He downed the last of the water in the bottle and looked at Hannah.

"At least an hour. It's been forty-five minutes so far." Hannah glanced at her phone. "I should text Luna. I hate inconveniencing her like this."

"I imagine she enjoys spending a few hours with Noah and Lucas."

"You're right. Luna is still practically a kid herself. And she loves the boys. Still, I want to be respectful of her time. Luna puts in a lot of hours at the bakery."

"She's young. That's why." He chuckled. "I'm guessing she's in her twenties."

"Yes. Twenty-five. Ten years younger than me."

"Same here," Rob said. Huh. He didn't realize that he and Hannah were the same age. Maybe that was why they got along so well.

Hannah typed on her phone. A smile curved her mouth and she typed again before looking up.

Rob couldn't help but stare. Hannah had a lovely smile.

"What did she say?" he asked.

"They're making cookies and having a great time."

"There you go. She's like an aunt to them." He smiled, recalling his own childhood. "I used to spend the weekend with my mom's sister every now and then. Great memories."

"It sounds like you're close to your family."

"Yeah, I'm an only child. I call my folks once a week. I haven't been home to New Hampshire in four years, though they visited me in Raleigh a couple of times."

"Four years. That's a long time. I take the boys to Beaumont to see my mom at least twice a month."

"Yeah, I guess it is. Humbolt is a small town. Though not as small as Tumbleweed. I keep meaning to go back. The timing is never right." He shrugged. Admittedly, it might never be right. Visiting Humbolt meant facing memories on every street corner and facing people who knew the truth about his past.

"Who's Tom Archer?" Hannah asked. "It's hard not to take notice of the fact that he keeps calling."

"Tom Archer." He took a deep breath. He should have realized that ignoring Tom's calls wouldn't make the situation go away.

"Tom is…was my brother-in-law. Cassidy was his sister. My wife."

"Are you avoiding him?"

Rob sighed and studied the deep cracks in the dry, red ground as he considered the question. A question he was loath to answer. He liked Hannah. More than he ought to. What would she think of him if he explained that he was to blame for his wife's death? Rob wasn't ready to see the disappointment on her face. It was bad enough that he saw it every single day when he looked in the mirror.

Yeah, he'd save that story for another day.

"I guess I am avoiding him," he admitted. "For now."

Hannah put a hand on his arm, her touch reassuring. He

met her gaze, saw compassion in her dark eyes. More compassion than he deserved.

"I'm sorry," she said softly. "That was thoughtless of me."

"No. It's fine. You didn't do anything wrong." He opened his mouth to explain just as a loud horn split the silence. A monster tow truck came into view. The truck's horn tooted another friendly greeting to announce its arrival. Dust swirled in the air as the vehicle drove past, emergency lights flashing, before the driver parked in front of the van.

A hefty man with the muscled girth of an offensive lineman jumped down, adjusted his worn ball cap, and headed toward them. A smile lit up his round face, growing wider as he approached. "Hey there, Pastor Rob." He offered a massive hand. "Good to see you, sir. You married my son last autumn. Buddy Tippens."

"Sure. I remember," Rob said as he shook the man's hand. As he recalled, Buddy was as muscled as his father. "Nice to see you again."

"I heard you had a birthday this week. Hope it was a good one."

Rob threw Hannah a look as he nodded. "It was. Thanks."

"I want you to know I encourage everyone to sit in the pew on Sundays. You've got a way with words, Pastor Rob. You aren't fancy. No sirree, you talk common sense about the Lord and the Bible."

Rob stared at the man as he spoke, surprised at the praise. "I, um…thank you."

"I'm just telling it like it is. Everyone in town says the same thing."

"Good to see you, Miss Hannah," the man said. "I trust we put enough rubber bands and bubble gum on your vehicle last time you were in the shop."

Hannah laughed. “Yes, it seems so. There’ve been no problems lately.”

The man nodded and turned to the tow truck. “I’ll get things hooked up, and have that van loaded onto my rollback in no time at all. Then, you two can jump in the front seat. Won’t take but ten, fifteen minutes, tops.”

“Sounds good,” Rob said. He handed over the keys. “Thanks for getting here so quickly.”

“My pleasure, sir. When dispatch said it was Miss Hannah and our good pastor, I hustled myself down here.”

“Thank you. I appreciate that,” Rob said.

“Least I can do.” He pointed over his shoulder to the van. “I’ll have a look.”

“Are you okay?” Hannah whispered to Rob.

“Kind of speechless, if I’m being honest.”

“Why?”

Rob looked at Hannah, searching for words to express how the man’s words had humbled him. “I’m not accustomed to such effusive praise,” he finally said.

“This is Texas. Effusive is our middle name.”

“What’s his name?” he asked.

“That’s Buddy Sr.,” she whispered. “Buddy Tippens Sr.”

“Right. Right. His son is Buddy Jr.?”

“Yes. Junior and his bride had their reception at the rodeo grounds outside of town. The entire church staff attended the barbeque.”

“Uh-huh, that wedding reception was my introduction to jalapeño peppers.” He recalled he’d only been in town a month and hadn’t gotten his bearings yet. Hannah had his back in those days and she still did.

Buddy whistled and shook his head, walking toward them. “What happened to the van? I mean besides the fact that this sad sack is already on its last legs and ready for the auto graveyard."

"Pothole and an armadillo," Rob said.

"That'll do it." Buddy nodded solemnly. "Glad you two are okay. Gonna be a challenge to get that on the flatbed with that tie rod situation."

"Do you want some help?" Rob asked.

"Naw, I've got it. This will take longer than I estimated. I'll call my son to pick you two up. He's only thirty minutes out."

Buddy jumped into the tow truck and reversed the vehicle until it was centered with the front of the van. He got out, donned heavy-duty gloves and pushed the left tire straight.

Rob stared, amazed as Buddy got back in the truck and inched the flatbed beneath the van. Every few inches he got out of the truck and repeated the process, pushing the tire straight.

"What's he doing?" Hannah asked.

"Proving why he needs to eat a good breakfast every morning." Rob crossed his arms. "That is one patient man."

Hannah turned to Rob. "What are we going to do about the boxes?"

"The only thing we can do. Empty the van at the auto repair shop and take the boxes in our cars to the church. The bigger question is how will our homebound folks get to church on Sunday?"

"That part I can handle. We have a church phone tree that's mainly used for inclement weather or prayers. Once we get back, I'll get the calls started. I have a list of the parishioners who are usually picked up for services."

"Somehow, I knew you would," Rob said.

"I should also send Luna an update." She fished around in her tote bag for her phone.

While she texted Luna, he looked at his cell. The voicemails from his office had been forwarded to his phone, including Tom's message asking him to call back.

Eventually, he'd call Tom. Yeah. Eventually.

Rob brought up the pictures he'd snapped in the field, a slow smile tugging at his mouth at the images of Hannah. Her dark waves of hair framed a heart-shaped face. The brown eyes radiated warmth, intelligence and a bit of sass. An irresistible combination. She didn't have a clue how beautiful she was—inside and out.

His heart clutched as he realized there wasn't anyone else he'd rather be stranded in the backwoods of Texas with. She'd become more than a good friend. When he wasn't paying attention, Hannah had found a way past his defenses and stood knocking at his heart. A heart that for the first time in four long years answered yes.

That worried him because, despite the praise Buddy Tippens had heaped upon him, Rob knew he hadn't finished paying penance for his mistakes. Eventually, he would have to tell Hannah that he'd made some unforgivable decisions four years ago.

Chapter Seven

Rob held the bakery door open for three smiling women entering as he exited. His other hand gripped his to-go coffee and a small bag with a chocolate croissant. As promised last week, he'd made visiting the bakery part of his Saturday routine. A quick run, followed by a stop home to clean up, then he'd stop by Sweet Dreams Bakery and chat with the locals before he put in a few hours working on his sermon.

Rob Sterling's Saturday Tumbleweed routine. He chuckled, liking the sound of that. The cloud that hung over him for so long had finally begun to dissipate, and his world had gone from gray to color. Hannah and the people in this town had done that.

The last woman in the group exiting the shop stopped in front of him. "Thank you, Pastor Rob, and happy birthday."

"Thank you very much."

Rob chuckled. He'd gotten quite a few comments on his T-shirt this week as he ran the track at the high school and then down Main Street. There were even more comments about his birthday. All from word of mouth, as the *Gazette* issue with the picture Dixie took wouldn't even come out until Monday.

News traveled fast back home in Humbolt, New Hampshire, but Tumbleweed, Texas, was faster. In the words of

Hannah, news spread faster than the local cowboys hitting the rodeo chute.

He didn't mind being a conversation starter. The important thing was that he'd interacted one-on-one with more folks in Tumbleweed lately than in the last six months.

Crossing the street, he noticed a new banner. This one had been hung on the gazebo and advertised the church Easter services. Rob headed down the sidewalk to the employee door where neon yellow daffodils lined the sidewalk from the church to the park and surrounded the gazebo. Overhead, the redbuds were in full bloom, their pink flowers scenting the air.

Shouts of laughter rang out as children played on a swing set in the park and kicked a ball across the grass while mothers sat on benches chatting.

Community. This was his community. The sight had Rob smiling again.

Spring had sprung, and Easter was a mere two weeks away. Hannah told him that the church ladies hosted an Easter egg hunt in the park every year on the day before the Sunday holiday. He looked forward to being there.

This would be his first Easter in Tumbleweed. His first Easter sermon with this community. The pews would be full. He was well aware some folks made the pilgrimage to church only once a year for their Easter duty. He'd be fibbing if he didn't admit he was nervous about the message he planned to deliver.

He continued to remind himself that he was merely the vessel. While most favored Christmas, with its pageantry and gift giving, Rob loved the message of Easter, which was the greatest gift of all. Except for that bunny, Easter was the least commercial church holiday, and he liked it that way.

Pausing outside the employee entrance to the church, Rob

glanced up at the boarded-up window. Naomi had assured him that the new stained glass would be installed in time for Easter. Another thing to look forward to.

"Pastor Rob!"

Rob turned at Lucas's voice. The boy ran up to him, grinning, his eyes full of joy. "I moved up to the next level at chess club today."

"Way to go." Rob offered him a high five. "Tell me all about it."

"I did what you said. I slowed down and thought about the moves before I took them."

"Threats and responses."

"Yeah." Lucas nodded. "Yeah, that's it. Threats and responses."

"Just like real life. We have to think through what we're doing and what will happen when we make a move."

Lucas grimaced, giving the window a quick glance. "Like throwing that rock at the window. Every time I see it, it reminds me of what I did."

"You've learned a lot since that window. If you asked God for forgiveness, then you should forgive yourself and move on."

Rob froze for a moment at the irony of his words before brushing them off. After all, his situation was very different from that of a ten-year-old boy's.

"You finished chess club early. Are you supposed to go to the bakery now?" he asked Lucas.

He hadn't seen Hannah at Sweet Dreams this morning and didn't want to ask. Lately, Luna had shown an inordinate interest in his friendship with Hannah. No use fueling that fire since he hadn't quite sorted it out himself.

"Mom is at the pantry, painting. She didn't work at Luna's today."

"She bought paint already?" The woman sure didn't waste time. He'd give her that.

"Yep. Mom says the color is called Dreamy White." He rolled his eyes. "Looks like regular white to me."

Rob chuckled. Hannah had discussed paint colors with him yesterday, peppering him with questions and a dozen paint samples that all looked exactly the same. The final decision was between Cloud White and Dreamy White. Rob had done his best to muster enthusiasm about the choices. When pressed to cast the deciding vote, he'd chosen the latter color.

"She's kinda cranky today," Lucas said.

"How come?"

"I dunno, but I can tell when she starts talking to herself under her breath."

Rob silently chuckled. He'd noticed that about Hannah, too. Never an unkind word, but she did a lot of muttering when she was agitated.

"I, um… Can I ask you a question?" Lucas said.

"Sure. Let's go inside." Unlocking the door, Rob stepped inside and disarmed the church alarm system. Lucas turned on the lights before they moved down the hall to Rob's office.

"Have a seat and tell me what's up."

"My dad called. He wants to pick up me and Noah at the pantry and go to his house for the weekend. He'll bring us back on Monday 'cause next week is spring break."

"That's great." Rob was thrilled to see the boy's father finally stepping up to fulfill his parental obligations.

"I'd rather paint the pantry." The words were a dull pronouncement, spoken with a dramatic sigh.

"Like you said. Spring break is next week. You'll be painting soon enough."

"I guess."

Rob moved the chess set from yesterday's session aside,

and placed his coffee, the pastry bag, and his phone on the desk. "What's the question, Lucas?"

"Do I have to go to my dad's?"

"You know that's not a question for me. You should talk to your mom." He paused. Talk to his mom about that, yes. However, Lucas was his friend and the least Rob could do was give the boy a chance to get things off his chest in a safe space. "Why don't you want to go?"

"I'm kinda mad at him." The boy furrowed his brow and gazed at the floor.

"Why are you kinda mad?"

"He canceled our last three visits."

Hurt translated to mad. He'd seen that often enough in his counseling sessions. This was a hurting child. Hurting enough to throw a rock through a church window.

"Do you know why you're mad?" Rob asked softly.

Lucas raised a shoulder with a slow shrug and a long sigh. "He and his new wife had a baby and forgot about me and Noah."

"When we first talked, the day you broke the window, you said you were mad at God for not answering prayer. Prayers that your dad would remember his visits with you and Noah. Sounds to me like that's happening."

"But he forgot us for months."

"I see your point." Rob nodded and decided to approach the issue from another angle that Lucas might be able to visualize. "Do you remember how we discussed strategy yesterday when we had our lesson after school?"

Lucas nodded.

"And I said that you have to think from the opponent's perspective."

"Uh-huh."

"What did I mean by that?"

"Trying to figure out what their next move will be."

"Correct. But that's not all. The strategy is also about seeing things from your opponent's eyes."

Confusion filled Lucas's eyes. They were dark eyes, like his mother. "I don't get it, Pastor Rob. What do you mean?"

Rob slid the chessboard closer with the white pieces on his side. Reaching out, he moved the pawn forward. "It means you don't make decisions based on your feelings alone. You have to see the situation from the other side of the chessboard."

Rob rotated the board so the white game pieces were on Lucas's side.

"Understand?"

"Yes, sir."

He paused. "Let me ask you this. Do you know anything about that baby?"

"I know she's a girl."

"You have a sister." Rob smiled. "That's pretty cool. Don't you think?"

Another shrug before Lucas looked at Rob with a small smile. "Yeah. I guess so."

"Do you know why your dad hasn't picked you up for the last three months?"

"No."

"How did you feel when he didn't pick you up?"

"I thought he didn't love me."

Rob let Lucas sit with those words for a moment, the silence stretching.

"Do you love your dad?"

After a long pause, Lucas gave a slow nod, his eyes shimmering with moisture. He swiped at his face with the sleeve of his shirt.

"Then maybe you could give your dad a chance to explain. To tell you why he made the moves he did." He looked at Lucas. "Seems to me you have a lot of questions without any answers."

Lucas nodded again.

"Sounds corny, but I learned a long time ago that life is a lot like chess. We have to take a minute to see things from the other side of the board. Give your dad a chance to explain his moves. Will you do that?"

"Yes."

Rob's cell phone vibrated against the surface of his desk. A glance at the screen identified a text message from Hannah. "It's your mom. She's looking for you."

Lucas stood.

"I'll text her that you're on your way."

"Thanks, Pastor Rob."

"You're welcome. And congratulations again on moving up a level. I'm proud of you."

A smile snuck across Lucas's face as he turned to leave.

Hannah had done a fine job raising the boy. Today's lesson was more challenging than any chess match, though Rob had no doubt Lucas would move to the next level there as well.

For long minutes, Rob sat at his desk, staring at his phone. What had he told Lucas? *Life is a lot like chess. We have to take a minute to see things from the other side of the board.*

Yeah, apparently, his situation wasn't much different from the ten-year-old's after all. The sobering thought had Rob reaching for his laptop.

He stared at the screen a long time, then started typing.

Tom,
My apologies for dodging your calls. If you have time in your schedule, maybe we can plan a time for you to visit.

I'd love to show you around Tumbleweed. I'd also like the chance for us to talk.
Rob

His entire hand trembled as he hit Send.

It was time to face his past and stop walking in circles if he wanted the future the Lord planned for him.

Hannah slapped the roller into the paint pan and attacked the wall with a vengeance. Up and down, with the roller extension, until her arm ached. It had been three days, yet Rob's words—about not being an optimist—continued to agitate her. She'd remind herself he'd apologized and she was overreacting, and then, like a thorn in her side, the entire conversation ran through her mind again.

She'd worked for the man nearly seven months now. Yet, Rob didn't really know her, did he? If he did, he'd realize that optimism was part of her DNA. As for the rest, well, she was a mom. Moms were always prepared. That was part of the mother credo. Always prepared. Like the Boy Scouts… or maybe it was the Royal Canadian Mounted Police. Whatever. She was always prepared and proud of it.

Cranky didn't begin to cover how she felt each time she replayed the conversation. To make things worse, she was starting to second guess her feelings.

Like that moment between them in the van? There seemed to be more and more of those moments of late. That couldn't be a good thing because there was no way she had room in her life for a relationship if that was what was on the horizon.

Except it wasn't. She'd probably imagined the entire thing.

"Hi there, Hannah."

The door to the shop was propped open to release the paint fumes. Hannah turned at the sound of Rob's voice. He looked good, as usual. Tall, dark and Clark Kent. She looked away, hoping he couldn't read her mind.

"Pastor Rob. Did you need something?" she asked. Head down, she carefully dipped the roller into the paint pan and started on the next section of wall.

"No. Thought I'd stop by and see if you needed any help." He looked around. "You've got the wallpaper removed and the walls prepped already?"

"Turns out the boys like ripping off wallpaper. They ripped, I prepped, and today I started painting."

"That's great." He was silent for a moment, then he asked, "You're not mad at me, are you?"

"No. Why would you say that?"

"That quote you posted Friday seemed a little less Hannah than usual, and you just called me Pastor Rob."

"What quote was that?"

"Remember, you don't have to attend every argument you're invited to."

Hannah's lips twitched, but she was determined not to smile. She wasn't mad but she wasn't happy about Rob's character assassination of her, either.

"Oh, that quote." She concentrated on the paint roller. "No. Not mad. Just a lot on my mind."

Rob cleared his throat. "So, ah, did the boys get off to their father's okay?"

"Lucas told you?"

"He did. We chatted for a bit."

"Thank you. John seems committed to seeing the boys regularly, which is wonderful. Though Lucas wasn't happy when I told him." She looked at Rob. "Whatever you said made a difference. Thank you."

"I just let him talk it out. Sometimes all a person needs is some time to vent and figure out what they're really feeling."

Hannah continued to paint as he talked. Rob was right, of course. His words applied to her as well. And it was difficult to stay annoyed at the man when he treated her boys so kindly.

Out of the corner of her eye, she noticed Rob walk over to the counter and move the drop cloth a bit.

"I brought you a sweet tea from the diner." He placed a tall, covered cup with a straw tucked in the top on the counter.

Hannah smiled to herself, and amended her thoughts. Rob treated the boys *and her* kindly. "That wasn't necessary but thank you," she said.

"Oh, it was. I owe you for lunch on Thursday."

"Thursday?" Then she remembered and laughed. Yes, despite the van debacle, Thursday had been a good day. And a cool glass of sweet tea would be good about now. Points for remembering she didn't take her tea like a Yankee.

She put down the roller and walked to the counter to claim the drink. After taking a long sip, the crankiness slid away.

"I ran into Ginger Jackson," Rob said. "The oatmeal, coconut, and chocolate cookie woman."

Hannah tried not to laugh. "Did she 'make' you another batch of cookies?"

"No, she was in the diner when I bought the tea. No cookies, but lots of questions."

"Yes. That's our Ginger." Hannah shook her head. "Word to the wise. Ginger moves information faster than a text message. Be very careful what you say to her unless you want all of Tumbleweed and half of the next three towns over to know."

"I suspected as much when she asked me if I was dating anyone special."

Hannah gasped. "She didn't! Ginger asked a pastor about his dating life?"

"Sure did. As we were standing next to each other at the

cashier. Pretty sure half the diner heard. There was a guffaw or two in the vicinity of Jim Stewart's booth."

"What did you say to her?"

"I told her all of God's children are special."

Hannah covered her face after she practically snorted iced tea through her nose at the response. "Well done."

Both Hannah and Rob looked up at the sound of a knock on the doorframe.

"Hi there, people," Luna said. Her assessing glance went from Hannah to Rob, who stood beside her at the counter. Hannah could practically see the gears moving in her friend's head. Fortunately, Luna was discreet. She'd wait until they were alone before she offered her unsolicited opinion.

"Hi, Luna," Rob said.

"Pastor." She shot him a coy smile. "I saw you cross the street." She handed him a pastry bag. "I had a few chocolate croissants left over, and I'm closed on Sundays."

"Thanks, Luna. This is really nice of you."

"I happen to be really nice," Luna said with a wink. "Just letting you know in case you have a friend you want me to meet."

He laughed out loud. "I'll keep that in mind."

Luna turned to Hannah. "Need any help painting, my friend?"

"No way I'd let you, even if I did. You started baking at three a.m.," Hannah said. "But you can stick around to chat, if you want."

"I do have some tea," Luna said, her eyes sparkling with mischief.

"Tea? What a coincidence. I brought tea, too," Rob said, looking confused, as he assessed Luna's empty hands.

Luna laughed and winked at Hannah. "Tea is slang for information."

"Oh, right. *Tea.* That's my cue to exit." His awkward smile told Hannah that he'd never heard of the term.

Rob headed to the door. "I guess I'll see you two later." He held up the bag. "Thanks again, Luna."

"My pleasure. Bye, Pastor Rob," Luna called. She turned to Hannah. "That man is so adorable. He had no idea what tea meant."

"He does now. And he's going to think I gossip."

"There is nothing wrong with me sharing information without biased commentary."

"What information?" Hannah walked across the room to assess the drying paint on the walls. It was best to pretend she wasn't invested in Luna's info. She'd have to pray for forgiveness later.

"I was in the post office, and I overheard Jim Stewart inviting Patty Wright to his cousin's art gallery opening in Houston. Sort of a big deal, apparently, if you're into that kind of thing."

"What did she say?"

"She said, sure, as long as he doesn't talk politics."

Hannah laughed. "I love Patty."

"Do you think something is going on with the two of them?" Luna asked.

"No." Hannah shook her head. "They're old friends. That's all."

"I don't know. They were in the bakery last Saturday, sitting at a table with the mayor and a few other town bigshots. Jim snuck a peek at Patty a couple of times. He looked at her like Pastor Rob looks at you sometimes."

Hannah stumbled at the words, nearly stepping into the paint pan. "What are you talking about? Rob doesn't look at me like anything. You have absolutely got to stop reading those romance novels. When was the last time you went on a date, missy?"

"I'll have you know that romance novels these days are about empowered women," Luna said. "I'm empowered enough to know there isn't anyone in this town I want to date."

"I'm going to make it my mission to find you a date so you'll stop bothering me about my love life."

"Does Pastor Rob have a brother?" Luna asked. "Preferably one who also rides a motorcycle and wears a leather jacket when he does."

"Rob? No. He's an only child."

Luna gasped and pointed a finger at Hannah. "You called him Rob."

"All the staff call him Rob. He asked us to."

"Hmm. If you say so."

Hannah stood back and looked at the wall once again, hoping to distract her friend. "What do you think of this color? This is called Dreamy White."

"Meh." Luna raised a slim shoulder. "More boring than dreamy, if you ask me."

"Boring? It's for a food pantry. It's not supposed to be chic."

"Hannah, boring is boring. Maybe we can find some fun things to put on the wall at the rummage sale," Luna said.

"I'd be insulted, except decorating is not my thing. I give you full rein."

"And I accept the challenge. I think we can go a little retro." She pointed to the top of the wall. "With that high ceiling, we could put up some floating shelves with vintage cooking utensils, maybe a butter churn, some old-fashioned eggbeaters, and a stack of nesting bowls." Luna looked around. "A wall with beadboard wainscoting would be cute, too."

"There's no money for beadboard wainscoting. That's why we're having a rummage sale."

"Have you even asked the hardware store to donate anything?"

Hannah frowned. "No."

"Why not? How do you think I could afford that cute striped wallpaper in the bakery? I made a deal with a decorator in Beaumont. She gave me the wallpaper at-cost, and in return, I put a link to her company on the front page of the Sweet Dreams Bakery website."

"The church website designer moved away. We're fortunate to borrow high school kids to do updates."

"I said I'd do a page for the food pantry for you. I'm not just a pretty face. Coding is my hobby. All you have to do is talk to local businesses."

"You're right, and shame on me for not thinking of that." Hannah shook her head. "I'm soliciting sponsors to buy paint and shopping bags. I never thought of bigger ticket items. My only excuse is that I sit with these people in the pew on Sunday. I've found that it's easier to ask for a sponsorship check than beadboard or a ceiling fan."

"Make a list. All they can say is no."

"That's what Rob said," she murmured. Maybe she ought to start asking for help more often.

"What did Rob say?" Luna cocked her head, confused.

"Luna, let me ask you something."

"Sure."

"Do you think I'm an optimist?"

"Is that a trick question?"

"Someone told me that I have a bad case of waiting for the other shoe to drop."

Luna's eyes rounded, but she didn't say anything.

Hannah sighed. "I guess you agree."

"What I think is that you are the sweetest, most joyful person I know. I also think that you spend much too much time worrying. Granted, you have good reason to be anxious, considering your history of being let down. I understand how challenging it is being a single mom, Hannah. You have to advocate for three people, not just you. Give yourself some grace."

"I appreciate your kind and tactful way of telling me that it's true." Hannah mulled for a moment. "How do I change that?"

"Casting your cares upon the Lord may seem simplistic." Her friend smiled. "But on the flip side, once you determine the worst-case scenario, all you have to do is ask yourself if your God is big enough to handle that scenario." Luna leaned closer. "Hint. He is. He always is."

Hannah nodded slowly. "How did you get to be so wise, Luna Perez?"

"The hard way, my friend. I started with nothing but my abuela's recipes and a dream. God told me to trust Him, and I did. Though it certainly wasn't easy. I get where you're coming from. However, in the end, it's always about Him. The more you trust the Lord, the more the boys will as well. They'll learn more from your example than your words."

"You're right. I know you're right. I've even had the same self-talk and then dismissed it, choosing to be annoyed instead." She sighed. "Thank you."

Hannah reached out to hug her friend, but Luna backed away laughing.

"Not so close. You have paint all over your arms and your shirt. You, Hannah Bryant, are a messy painter."

"Oops." Hannah wiped her hands with a paint rag, succeeding in spreading even more paint all over.

"I better go," Luna said. "My best boy is waiting for me at home, and he's overdue for kibble."

"Give Roscoe a hug from me."

"I will." She gave a wave of her fingers. "Later, chica."

Hannah leaned against the counter and sipped the sweet tea Rob had brought her. Outside the window, the town moved by. Maybe she'd clean up, go home, tend to the horses, and watch a sappy movie on television. It was going to be very lonely without her boys around this weekend.

She wasn't used to being alone. At this stage in her life, she always thought there would be someone to cuddle with on the couch. A companion to share her hopes and dreams with.

And for a few fleeting and ridiculous moments she'd even hoped that person might be Rob.

Chapter Eight

Rob settled onto his couch with a bowl of popcorn and the remote. He'd watch a little Saturday college basketball before turning in. Tomorrow would be a long day, with two services, and he could use the rest before the big day.

When his phone rang, he searched for the device and finally found it stuck between the cushions. The number came up as Beaumont Regional Hospital. That couldn't be good.

Hand gripping the cell, he pressed the green button. "Pastor Rob Sterling here."

"Sir, we have a patient in the emergency department who would like to speak with you."

Oh, no. Rob tensed, his stomach lurching. He'd been in this business a while, yet nothing ever prepared him for phone calls from the police or hospitals, delivering unfortunate news. It never got easier, either.

"Rob, it's Hannah."

"Hannah?" He jumped up from the couch nearly knocking his popcorn bowl over. "What happened? Are you okay? Are the boys all right?"

"The boys are fine, I hope. I'm sorry to bother you. My phone died and…" She huffed. "What I'm trying to say is that I can't reach Luna, and I need a ride home."

"From the Beaumont Hospital."

"Correct. The medical clinic in Tumbleweed was closed, so

I drove to the nearest emergency room. I thought there would be less traffic in Beaumont than in Houston." She sighed. "I'm babbling. Would you be able to pick me up?"

"From the emergency room."

"I hurt my wrist. They tell me that I have a nondisplaced fracture. No surgery, just a cast."

"How did you get to Beaumont?"

"I figured Beaumont would be less busy than Houston, so I came here." She paused. "Did I already say that?" Another long pause.

"Hannah, how did you get there?"

"I drove."

"You drove! With a broken wrist?" Flummoxed, Rob raced to the closet to grab a jacket, then fumbled around searching for the keys to his car.

"My phone has died, so if you have a problem getting here, call the hospital number." Another pause. "Did I already say that? They gave me a shot when I first got here and I'm still a little woozy. For some reason, I'm not allowed to drive myself home."

"Thank you, Lord, for that," he muttered.

"Did you say you can pick me up?" she asked.

"Yes. I need the particulars."

Hannah gave him the address while he dug in his laundry basket for his keys.

"Drive carefully," she said. "There's a lot of traffic."

Drive carefully? Rob opened his mouth to ask her a dozen more questions and then stopped. "I'm on my way." He could ask questions later.

The drive to Beaumont took a lot less time than Rob remembered it taking in the past, though he kept his eye on the speedometer. It would take fast-talking to the church board if the police blotter section of the *Gazette* featured his mug shot.

Instead, he prayed for Hannah and any armadillos with the misfortune of being in his path tonight.

Forty minutes later, the sun completed its descent as Rob turned into the hospital drive, where gloomy shadows stretched from the parking lot to the massive building. Turning right, he pulled into the circular drive of the emergency department. Lights from the overhang lit up the busy entrance where people moved in and out through the automatic doors.

His gaze landed on a forlorn figure standing inside the ER, looking out through the big window. Rob hit the brakes. He jumped out and raced inside.

When Hannah turned to greet him, the white cast peeked out from beneath her jacket. His heart plummeted at the sight of his dynamic and self-sufficient secretary and friend injured and vulnerable.

"Oh, Hannah, what happened?"

"I miscalculated my reach on the ladder in the pantry."

"Does it hurt?" What a dumb question. Of course, it hurt.

"Not as much as it did. I have a prescription for pain pills they filled for me."

Rob swallowed hard, resisting the urge to take her in his arms and tell her he'd never let another shoe drop. Ever.

Instead, he escorted her out to his car, tucked her carefully into the passenger seat, eased the seat belt across her, and fastened the buckle.

She held up her phone. "Do you have a charger? I'm concerned the boys may have tried to reach me."

"Sure." He took her phone and plugged it into his car charger. "I'm going to go check on something," he said. "Be right back." Rob raced through the automatic doors and out of Hannah's line of vision. After a quick internet search on his phone, he tapped in the phone number of Sweet Dreams Bakery and prayed that Luna would answer.

"Hello?"

"Luna, this is Rob Sterling."

"Pastor, you sound different. Is everything all right?"

"I'm fine. Hannah broke her wrist. She fell off the ladder painting the pantry. I'm driving her home from the hospital in Beaumont. She has a cast and pain pills, but she's going to need help. And the boys won't be back until Monday."

"That's why Hannah called me earlier. Mystery solved. I was in my garden and missed her. She didn't answer when I returned the call."

"Listen, we're going to have to buddy up on this situation," Rob said. "Hannah will tell us she's fine and doesn't need help. She does."

"Got it. The bakery is closed on Sunday and Monday. I'll camp out on her couch."

"Thanks, Luna."

"That's what friends are for, right?"

"Right."

"Beaumont, huh? That puts your ETA at about forty minutes. I know where she keeps her key hidden. Roscoe and I will be waiting at her house."

"Roscoe? Your boyfriend?"

"My dog."

Rob chuckled, finally able to relax a bit. Between him and Luna, they'd take care of Hannah.

"And Pastor?" Luna said.

"Yeah?"

"You're the good friend of my good friend. That makes you my good friend as well. I anticipate many more chocolate croissants in your future."

He laughed at the logic. "Thanks. See you soon, Luna."

"Wait, what about the pantry? Should I go check on it?"

"I drove by on my way here. The shop looks like a struggle took place. I turned off the lights and locked the door." The emergency room doors swished open again. "Gotta go. She's in the car."

When he returned to his vehicle, Hannah was fast asleep, her face serene. Her dark waves were tangled, and Rob gently pushed them back off her face.

His heart tugged when she stirred. Hannah opened her eyes and blinked, looking straight into his soul. "Are you okay?" she asked.

"Me? I'm good."

Hannah gave a nod and closed her eyes again.

"Oh, Hannah," he whispered. "What have you done to me?"

The drive back to Tumbleweed was quiet. While Hannah dozed, Rob replayed the last six and a half months over and over in his head. At what point had he come to care for Hannah? How had she managed to inch her way into his heart?

Luna and a massive mutt sat on Hannah's porch when they finally arrived back in Tumbleweed. The animal appeared to be a cross between a horse and a Labrador retriever. Luna put down the book in her hand and rushed down the steps with the dog close behind, dragging his leash.

Rob quietly got out of his car and eyed the animal. "Roscoe, I presume."

"Yes." Luna peeked in the passenger window. "Oh, she's asleep. Are you going to carry her? That would be so chivalrous."

"She broke her wrist, not her leg." Rob frowned. "Plus I can't see any scenario where Hannah would let me carry her."

Luna chuckled. "Okay, fine. I guess you're right. What are the doctor's instructions?"

"Elevate the arm, ice it twenty minutes at a time. They filled her pain prescription at the hospital pharmacy. Enough to get her through twenty-four hours. Then she's supposed to use over-the-counter meds."

"Got it. I have ice packs at my place."

Roscoe barked and Hannah opened her eyes. "Hiya, Roscoe," she murmured with a goofy smile.

Luna and Rob assisted Hannah up the steps and into the house. "Come on, sweetie," Luna said. "Let's get you in bed."

"Where are the boys?" Hannah asked, looking around, disoriented.

Rob handed Hannah's phone to Luna. "Asleep at their dad's," he said.

Hannah nodded and followed Luna into the bedroom.

Roscoe sat in the middle of the living room, his soulful gaze following Rob as he paced the floor. "What?" Rob asked the dog.

Roscoe whined and approached, knocking his massive head into Rob's knees.

"Seriously? You want attention. Now?"

The dog whined again, knocking into Rob once more.

"Fine." He rubbed the dog's huge floppy ears and gave him a chin rub, massaging the jowls. Roscoe sighed blissfully.

"Roscoe likes you," Luna said with a smile.

"I'm guessing Roscoe likes everyone."

"That's not true." Luna cocked her head toward the front door. "I forgot my charger and my headphones. I'm going to run to my house and grab them and a few ice packs. I'll be right back."

"Don't rush," Rob said.

"She's sound asleep," Luna said. "You can go ahead and leave. I know you have a sermon to give tomorrow."

"I'll wait until you get back." He took off his glasses and ran a hand over his face. The sermon was ready, though he didn't think he'd get much sleep tonight, anyhow.

Luna stared at him, then offered a small, knowing smile

that Rob absolutely refused to address. She turned to the dog. "Stay, Roscoe. Mommy will be right back."

"Wait. Aren't you taking Roscoe with you?"

"Nah, it's good for him to do some male bonding. Right now, his only guy friend is the mailman, and I suspect he's seeing the poodle down the street on the side."

"You're funny, Luna."

She pushed her dark braid over her shoulder. "Funny ha-ha or funny odd?"

"You have a great sense of humor."

"Right." Luna rolled her eyes. "That's what my brother used to say when he tried to get me a date for the prom. My sister is funny and bakes a mean loaf of sourdough."

"I'm sure there's a guy out there that's waiting for a funny girl with a loaf of sourdough."

"Your lips to God's ears." Luna tossed her keys into the air as she moved toward the door. "You're absolutely sure you don't have a cousin or something?"

"I'll ask my mother."

"Do that." Luna paused and looked at him. "You can't fight it much longer, Pastor Rob," she said softly.

"Fight what?"

She raised her brows and nodded toward the bedroom, with an expression that said "don't play dumb with me, mister."

He opened his mouth to protest but instead shrugged. "You know, you can't get back here if you never leave. Right?"

She laughed and pushed open the screen door.

"Come on, boy." Rob reached for Roscoe's leash. "Let's go take a walk in the yard."

Lit only by the moonlight and a canopy of stars, the cattails surrounding the pond swayed in the slight breeze. A cricket frog's high-pitched mating call mingled with the sound of Big W Ranch cattle in the distance. Rob stood at the rough-hewn fence that surrounded the pond for minutes, listening to the chorus.

Roscoe tugged on the leash, and Rob followed the animal as he sniffed every last scent in the yard.

Rob shook his head, still contemplating Luna's words. She was wrong. There was no fight going on within him. Common sense told him that Hannah deserved the best, but he wasn't sure he could deliver that best. Luna had given him something to think about—that much was clear.

If Luna could see his heart on his sleeve, who else in town could?

Eventually, he had to chat with Hannah about his past. After the rummage sale and all the Easter festivities. When things calmed down in Tumbleweed.

Maybe then he could tell her about his mixed-up feelings and let her decide if she wanted to take a chance on a guy with too many regrets.

"What do you mean, I'm on light duty?" Hannah put her hands on her hips and winced. She kept forgetting about the cast. She looked down at Rob who stood in her yard, inspecting the gas grill.

The scene seemed surreal. Rob Sterling had taken over the grill at her house. Pastor Rob. Her boss was going to cook hot dogs for lunch.

"I read your paperwork from the hospital," Rob said. He waved the grill scrubber in the air as he spoke. "The physician was very clear. After the first twenty-four hours, try to use your hand and wrist as normally as possible."

Hannah mustered as much patience as she could. "Yes. Today is Monday. It's been twenty-four hours. We're saying the same thing."

"Are we? I'm pretty sure I said that you're on light duty." He paused and then nodded. "Yeah, that's what I said."

"Potato. Potahto," she said with a shrug.

"Hannah, as your employer, I'm telling you that what you do at the church office is not normal. However, starting tomorrow, it will be. No painting at the pantry. No climbing ladders. No lifting donation boxes and carrying them to the storage room, and absolutely no moving penny-farthing bicycles."

"Penny-farthing, what?" Luna looked up from where she sat on the porch reading a book. Her glance moved from Rob to Hannah.

"Penny-farthing," Rob said. "One of those old-fashioned bicycles with the giant front wheel."

Luna set her book aside and stood up. "Come on," she said to Hannah. "You may as well give up. Let's go in the house and get things ready for lunch."

"Do I have time to hit a few baseballs with the boys?" Rob asked.

"Sure," Luna said. "We just have to decide which of the fifty salads in the fridge we're having with lunch."

"Are you leaving Roscoe out here?" Rob asked.

"Yes, boys outside, girls inside," Luna said.

Once they were in the house. Hannah peeked out the window where Lucas and Noah stood in the field pounding their fists into the new mitts Rob bought them, waiting for Rob to hit a baseball to one of them. She laughed when Noah chased after a high fly ball with Roscoe right behind him.

Maybe it was time to think about getting a dog. Hannah grimaced. Was there really room for another ball in her juggling act? Still, she'd moved them all to the country so they could have things like wide open spaces and animals.

"How are things going with their father?" Luna asked.

"Fine. John dropped them off this morning while you and

Rob were gone. I don't understand it, but I guess praying for his new wife and baby was the right approach."

"Now they have two dads."

"Luna! Shhh!" Hannah whirled around.

"What?" Luna poked her head into the refrigerator and pulled out a bag of carrot sticks. She wandered over to the window and stood next to Hannah, munching on a carrot.

"Rob is a friend. Pastor Rob. That's all."

"He really cares about them," Luna observed. "It's obvious."

"I know," Hannah said on a sigh. She still wasn't sure if that was a good thing.

"He cares about you as well. Did I tell you that he refused to leave last night when I had to go to my house for my phone charger? I've never seen such devotion on a man's face." She chuckled. "Except for Roscoe. He has the same expression when it's dinnertime."

"Rob has been pretty wonderful." Hannah smiled, thinking about this morning. "He mowed the lawn when you went home for a bit. Then he left and stopped by the grocery store for some things he decided I needed. He came back all cleaned up with baseball mitts for the boys." She was supposed to buy mitts, but Rob beat her to it. It was hard to fault the man for being so caring.

"Lucas and Noah could do worse than two men in their lives."

"Yes. You're right." Hannah sighed again. "The thing is, Rob will be leaving in the fall."

"For sure?" She shot Hannah a skeptical glance.

"He only signed on for a year. Why would he stay?"

"Lots of reasons. Like the fact that he fits in like he was born here. I hardly even notice that New Hampshire accent anymore."

Hannah laughed. "You're right about that. I've gotten used to it as well. I nearly fell over the first time I heard him order *chowda* at the diner last year. He noticed me trying not to giggle and immediately informed me that *fixin' ta* isn't a word, either."

"Of course it is," Luna said. "And so is *y'all*, *yonder* and *pea-pickin'*."

Hannah opened the refrigerator, with hopes of distracting Luna from the topic at hand. "Will you look at this? Every time I open the refrigerator I'm stunned. Are you the one who activated the meal train?"

"No, that was Patty Wright." Luna glanced at the counter. "If you're going to complain, I'll gladly take that pecan pie off your hands."

"No way." She shook her head. "Isn't that Patty something? She sent one of her ranch hands over to take care of the horses yesterday and today and had them fetch my car in Beaumont. Said it was her honor to help out."

"I know how difficult it is for you to accept help, Hannah, but you have to remember that when someone blesses you, the Lord blesses them. I have no idea if that's a Biblical truth or not but my abuela said it to me a thousand times growing up." Luna put her hand on Hannah's arm. "Don't deny your friends a blessing."

"I never thought of it that way." Hannah smiled. "Louise and Dixie are blessed as well, then. They've dropped off flowers and a card signed by the church ladies."

"That reminds me," Luna said. "Do you get the *Gazette*?"

"No. I read the issue that's delivered to the church."

"Today is Monday. Guess whose picture is on the front page. Clark Kent. Above the fold, no less." Luna pulled the paper out of her purse. "It was on my porch when I went back to the house for Roscoe's kibble this morning."

Hannah laughed at the picture. "That is too cute."

Luna read the caption out loud. "Beloved Pastor Rob Sterling of Tumbleweed Community Church, holding up his birthday T-shirt." Luna shook her head. "I'm sorry I missed that party."

"Miss Luna, come out here," Rob called. "I need a break to start lunch. The boys claim you can play ball. Let's see what you got."

"I'll be right there," Luna called through the screen. She gave Hannah the bag of carrots.

Rob held the door for Luna as he entered the kitchen. "Just try to avoid the pond."

Luna glared at him.

"What are you reading?" he asked Hannah, leaning close to take a peek.

He smelled like grass, springtime and fresh air. Her favorite things. Hannah stepped back from her favorite things and handed him the paper. "Here you go."

Rob groaned. "I look goofy as can be."

"No. You look good. I'm guessing this will ignite another round of casseroles."

"Don't even say that." He grabbed a paper towel, removed his glasses and wiped his face. "I don't think I'll ever get used to this weather. What is it, a hundred and twenty degrees out there? In March, no less."

"You might be exaggerating. The temperature is only seventy-five."

"The humidity must be at least eighty percent right now."

"Don't you have humidity in New Hampshire?"

"Not in March. And if we do, it still isn't like here in Texas. Mind if I grab a bottle of water?"

"Go ahead. They're tucked behind six hundred casseroles."

"Ah, I see the hot dogs in here, too." Rob grabbed the hot dogs and put them on the table. Then, he pulled out a bottle of water, took the lid off, and practically downed the entire bottle before relaxing against the counter.

This might be a good time to plead her case again, while he was off guard. Hannah reviewed her strategy and cleared her throat. "I really would like to finish painting the pantry, Rob. You know, I paint with my right hand."

"Then how did you break your left one?"

"Trying to break my fall."

He nodded slowly as though thinking the matter through. "So if you trip or something, you'd land on your broken wrist."

She shook her head. "That's highly unlikely. Louise would probably tell you it's statistically impossible."

Rob laughed. "Nice try. The boys and I are going to finish painting the pantry."

"You don't need to. I am perfectly capable of…"

He clucked his tongue. "Too late. I've already rearranged my schedule. Did that this morning."

"Did you sync the church calendar with your calendar?"

"I did, yes."

He crossed his arms, looking much too handsome for his own good, in jeans and a T-shirt, his dark hair slightly mussed. She wasn't accustomed to so much masculinity in her kitchen.

"Hannah, have you ever asked yourself why you have the need to do it all yourself?"

Uh-oh. Already she didn't like this line of questioning. "Maybe I'm just a perfectionist."

"Maybe, but I think it goes back to our previous discussion."

"Which discussion?"

She saw the look on his face. "Oh, *that* discussion."

"Yep. You expect others to let you down. If you do it yourself, then there's no chance of that happening."

"I…" She didn't know what to say.

"There are two takeaways here, Hannah."

"Is this a sermon?"

"I'm serious. First, let me assure you that people will let

you down. We've fallen from grace. It's going to happen. Deal with it. Your life will be a whole lot easier. So will Lucas and Noah's."

"Second?"

"I'm your friend. Luna's your friend. You can tell from your refrigerator that you have lots of friends. We aren't any of us perfect, but we all have one thing in common. We care for you. You don't have to do everything yourself. Let us in."

Ouch! The truth definitely hurt. She didn't care for the picture of herself he had painted.

Silence stretched.

"Okay?" he asked softly.

"I'll work on that," she said.

"Let the boys help you. It truly is an honor for them to serve their mother. Don't deny them that privilege."

The words were very reminiscent of Luna's abuela's advice on blessings. Obviously, the Lord thought she needed a remedial class on the topic. He was right. She'd become too stubborn and set in her ways over the years. It was time for a change.

"You're right," Hannah replied.

Rob smiled and gently took her hand. "Now, would you please direct me to the hot dog rolls? I'm starving and the grill is hot and ready to go."

Hannah nodded, unable to form a coherent sentence when he was touching her.

She pointed him in the direction of the hot dog buns, then opened the refrigerator, letting the frigid temperatures cool her flushed face.

One thing was certain: It was getting more and more difficult as the days and weeks went by to hide how she felt about Rob Sterling.

Chapter Nine

The sun rose at 7:13 a.m. on the second day of the Tumbleweed Community Rummage Sale. Rob foolishly assumed he'd be the first volunteer to arrive as the last pink streaks of sunrise melted from the sky.

But he wasn't even close to first. Louise and her pink-vested infantry were everywhere, toting boxes and prepping tables for today's sale.

Even Hannah arrived before he did and had already set up a table with a pink-and-black banner with the words Sweet Dreams Bakery. The table held a giant insulated container of coffee and one for hot water, with a container of tea bags close by. There was also an assortment of mini-muffins and mini-cinnamon rolls.

She smiled as he approached and his heart caught. One little smile from Hannah could make a guy's day.

"Good morning. How about a cup of coffee courtesy of Sweet Dreams Bakery?"

"Yes, please." He looked up at the sky. "We've been blessed with great weather two days in a row."

"The power of prayer," Hannah said. She slid a cup of black coffee and a white pastry bag across the table with her right hand. "Chocolate croissant. I snagged one for you."

"Thank you." Rob tucked the bag into the pocket of his jacket.

"You're welcome."

"What is all this?"

"Luna's idea. She donated everything. The plan is to lure people inside the fence for the final day. Folks have to buy a ticket to get inside the fence for free coffee and a pastry."

"That Luna is a savvy businesswoman." He glanced at her cast, which was now neon pink. "You went to the doctor?"

She raised a palm in gesture. "I didn't drive there. Luna took me for my follow-up yesterday after the rummage sale closed down for the day."

"I would have driven you."

"I appreciate that, but Luna had to do some shopping in Beaumont anyhow."

"What did the doctor say?"

"It's healing well. I told him that was because my boss wouldn't let me do anything. I was rewarded with this pretty cast that will match my Easter dress."

"You'll glow in the dark now." He looked around. "Where are the boys?"

"Noah has choir practice with Henry. Lucas is bringing out the last of the donation boxes from the storage room before he heads to chess club. What a relief it will be to have the room back."

"I agree. Did you notice the accordion and penny-farthing sold?"

"Yes. Do you know who bought them? This place was wall-to-wall people yesterday. I tried to keep my eye on a few pieces out of curiosity, but my table was so busy I hardly had time to sit down."

"We had a couple of antique dealers from Houston here in the afternoon. They said the prices were dirt cheap. One of them wheeled in a cart. He filled it up and headed to a rental truck parked down by the gazebo."

"We'll see that bike again in an antique store in Houston marked up at double the price for city folks. They're going to make a killing, thanks to us," Hannah said.

"Okay by me. As long as we reach our quota." He looked over at Ron Garcia, who had just set up the ticket table at the front entrance. "I should check and see how we did yesterday. Maybe slashing prices to fifty percent off today isn't such a good plan, after all."

"Please do. I gauge my hard-sell spiel on how the money is flowing."

"You do a hard sell?"

Hannah shot him an indignant look. "I can be a hardnose when necessary."

Rob laughed. He strolled over to the money man, who sat counting bills. "Morning, Ron. Do you think fifty percent off all sales is a good plan for today?"

"I absolutely do. It was Louise's idea, and I concur. It will bring back yesterday's customers who weren't persuaded to part with their cash." Ron stopped counting money and looked at him. "Besides, come two o'clock today, the last thing we want is to have to haul this stuff to the thrift store or into a moving truck."

"True. We were blessed with sunshine and a breeze yesterday. The same is forecast for today. I would have hated to lug all this to the high school gym if it rained."

"You are right, Pastor Rob. We were blessed." Ron smiled and leaned closer, looking around to be sure he wasn't overheard. "This is just between you and me for now, but with the matching donations anticipated from the Big W Ranch and Stewart Properties, we made enough money to pay off the loan yesterday. Today is gravy."

"Thank you, Lord," Rob said.

"Amen," Ron concurred. "We'll wait until the next board

meeting to figure out how to allocate the extra funds, but I assume repairs on the van are at the top of your list."

"Yes, though I have another issue I'll take up with the board later." Rob nodded. That issue was a pay increase for the church secretary. "Thanks, I appreciate everything you've done, Ron."

"Don't thank me. We need to motivate Jim and Patty more often. If you recall, they agreed to match what we raised here out of pure competitive spirit. We could build the school a new soccer field if we work this right next year." He winked at Rob and nodded to Patty's pies set up a few tables away. "Those pies alone brought in enough cans to stock the pantry for a week."

Rob strolled over to where Jim stood, eyeing the pies Patty pulled from a cardboard box and arranged on the table. Like the other church ladies, Patty wore a pink vest. As usual the widowed rancher had a smile and a kind word for everyone.

Patty swatted at Jim's hand when he rearranged a pie on her table. "Hands off the merchandise. You touch the pie, you buy the pie."

Well, almost everyone.

"How many pies did you buy yesterday, Jim?" Rob asked.

Patty had posted a sign stipulating ten cans would get the buyer one of her famous pies. It was a steep price, though not a single person balked.

"Oh, a few," he mumbled.

"He bought ten," Patty said. "Came in here with two wheelbarrows full of canned goods for the pantry."

"You can freeze the pies," Jim said. "I like to have them around when company stops by. I've got more canned goods in my car." He raised a brow, a smile appearing. "Might donate more today and make it an even dozen pies and annoy Patty at the same time."

Rob chuckled. "No crime in a genuine appreciation of pecan pies. I picked up a couple myself." Although Rob couldn't help but wonder if Jim's appreciation was for the pie baker, not just the pies.

"You fellas might consider talking less and working faster," Louise said from behind them. Rob turned around to greet the mayor, who not only wore a pink vest that said Boss Lady on the lapel—today, but she'd also added a pink felt cowboy hat with a band of faux crystals.

"Nice hat, Louise," Rob said.

"Thanks, I picked it up right here at the rummage sale. Buy local, you know." She tapped the clipboard in her hand loudly with a pen and shot a pointed look at Jim. "We've got trash receptacles that need bags and 'Fifty percent off' signs that have to be posted on every table."

"We don't open for another forty minutes," Jim countered. "What's the hurry? I'm still recovering from yesterday."

"Why, Jim Stewart, you're the same age I am. Are you aware that four out of the five most chronic diseases can be prevented with regular exercise?" Louise continued. "I suggest you grab a cup of coffee and a couple of ibuprofen and get moving."

Someone called her name, and the mayor dashed off across the parking lot.

"Regular exercise. I guess that includes jabbering," Jim groused. "She sure is bossy."

Rob nodded, suspecting that Louise had been bossy all her life. Pretty much as bossy as Jim.

"Pastor Rob, have you got a minute?"

Rob turned around to find Buddy Tippens Sr. waving at him. He stepped outside the fence to meet him on the sidewalk. "Buddy, I hope you're here with good news about the church van."

"Good news and bad news. Which do you want first?" Buddy did his usual hat dance, taking off his faded cap and then slapping it back on while waiting for a response.

"I prefer to get the bad news out of the way."

"Well, sir, we're waiting on a part for the van. As you can imagine, locating parts for a vehicle of that…maturity can be challenging. My team searched the internet for the part we needed and finally located one. They're shipping it from a country whose name I can't even spell. That means you won't have it for Easter Sunday service. My apologies, sir."

"I appreciate the effort you've put into this. But I have to tell you, that's not good news at all. Last Sunday was chaotic. There are too many folks needing rides and not enough volunteers. A few of our volunteers turned out to be directionally-challenged. I had one group that ended up at the Dairy Queen between here and Beaumont. They never did make it to service."

"Now you're gonna tell me they were never heard from again. We call that a tall tale in these parts." Buddy laughed long and hard, his eyes watering.

When Rob didn't respond, Buddy frowned. "You're joshing with me, right?"

"If only I were."

"I guess that makes the good news even sweeter," Buddy said. "I've got a second cousin on my mother's side who manages a dealership in Houston. He owes me a favor or six, and I called them in."

Buddy tucked his hands in the back pockets of his jeans. "Look yonder, over there, parked beside the gazebo. The silver van."

"Wow." Rob assessed the shiny passenger van. It practically sparkled in the morning sunshine. "Nice vehicle, but too expensive for our church budget."

"Nah, this is a loaner. Until the church van is repaired. Seats sixteen. Your old clunker seats twelve. Of course, that means you have to have a special license to drive it. I'm guessing someone in the congregation can do that."

"I'll head to the motor vehicle place and get myself that license right away," Rob said, excitement growing.

Buddy held out the keys. "I guess that means you're okay with it?"

Rob took the keys and pocketed them. "Buddy, it means that I believe you're an answer to prayer."

"Hah. Not me, but the good Lord. We'll get everyone to church on Easter Sunday and then some."

"Buddy, seriously. You're amazing. Thank you."

"No problem. Happy to help. By the way, I saw you tooling down Main Street in your little compact the other day."

"Yeah, that's my rainy-day vehicle."

"Pastor, you're in Texas now." Buddy grimaced. "No offense intended, but your vehicle looks like it only has a few breaths left in it. Big fella like you needs a four-by-four. My cousin can get you a deal on a shiny black pickup with all the bells and whistles."

"What am I going to do with bells and whistles?"

"Enjoy them. That's what. Why, my truck heats my back, has an ultrasonic deer whistle, can speak four different languages, and reminds me to take my blood pressure pill."

But did it have an armadillo early warning system? Rob smiled at the thought. "That sure is something. I appreciate the offer, and I'll give it some thought."

"Fair enough."

"Thanks again, Buddy, and thank your cousin for me."

"Will do. See you in church, Pastor Rob."

"Yes. You know where to find me."

Rob gave the van a final longing look. Imagine a brand-new church van delivered to his front door. The Lord had a hand in this, and he couldn't wait to tell Hannah. Only someone stuck on a dirt road for two hours after nearly running into an armadillo would appreciate this like he did.

He smiled, recalling the day. There was a moment when he forgot that he was the guy with a shadow following him and a shaky future in front of him. He'd almost given in to the urge to kiss Hannah.

That would have been a mistake and a dishonorable decision until they'd talked. Things were going well, and he more than suspected it was time to put his heart and his past on the table.

As Rob returned to the rummage sale, Lucas came out of the church struggling with two big boxes that hid the top of his body. "Let me take those for you," Rob said.

"Thanks, Pastor Rob."

"How many boxes are left?"

"This is it."

"Great. Grab a muffin from your mom's table before you head off to chess club. And remember what we talked about yesterday during our session. *Use your pawn wisely.*"

"*Because the pawn is the heart of the game,*" Lucas said with a grin. He nodded and ran around the sidewalk to his mother's table.

The ear-piercing screech of a whistle had Rob picking up his pace. Louise had sounded the warning. Fifteen minutes until the gate opened. Folks were already lining up at the entrance. Several waved at him and called out a greeting.

Rob waved back. He glanced up and down Main Street, where folks window-shopped and hurried into Sweet Dreams Bakery before Luna ran out of her famous cinnamon rolls.

In the park, children chased each other. The American

flag planted next to the gazebo waved in the morning breeze. Rob took a deep breath, appreciating the scene before him.

Tumbleweed had grown on him. Every building, every person.

Could he see himself settling down in this cozy Texas town? Absolutely. Except that wasn't up to him.

His next steps were up to the Lord.

"Look, Luc. Look how dark it is outside," Noah said. "I've never had pizza so late. This is fun."

Hannah turned from the sink, where she washed a couple of plates and glasses. "It is late. It took a long time to get things broken down from the rummage sale." She looked over at Rob, who'd just finished off his third slice. "It looks like you approve of the celebration pizza."

He nodded. "Excellent pizza. I had no idea you could find good pizza in Texas."

Hannah could only laugh. "You're having all kinds of firsts lately aren't you?"

"You know what?" he said. "I am. And it feels good."

"What are we celebrating?" Lucas asked. He peeked into one of the pizza boxes on the kitchen counter and helped himself to another slice before sliding into his chair once more.

"The pantry. The one you and Noah and Pastor Rob spent all week painting and cleaning up and wouldn't let me get near." She eyed Rob, who silently laughed.

"Uh-huh," Lucas said.

"We raised enough money to pay the rent on the building for the next year. The pantry is all ours for twelve months. That means that we can take donations and buy food to fill the shelves."

Rob looked at Hannah. "The fact that we raised the money was definitely the good Lord's doing, but I'd like to give credit where it belongs. You, Hannah Bryant, never stopped believing that this project would be a success."

"You had faith in the project, too," she protested.

He chuckled. "Oh, I think it would be fair to say that I've been on a roller coaster the last thirty days. You cast all your cares on Him. What an example you are for your boys and the community."

Hannah's face warmed at his words. "Thank you," she murmured.

"Go, Mom," Lucas said. "We're proud of you."

"Thank you, honey."

"Who's the pantry for?" Noah asked. He pushed his plate back and wiped his mouth with a napkin.

Hannah nodded to Rob to chime in with an explanation.

"The church family," he said. "Our job at Tumbleweed Community Church is to feed people. We feed their soul, and when they need it, we feed their stomachs, too."

"I don't get it. Why don't they buy their own food?" Noah asked.

"Good question, Noah," Rob said. "Sometimes people lose their jobs, or their car breaks down, or they get sick. When emergencies happen, you might not have enough money left to buy food for your family."

"Does the pantry give food to people who need to make dinner?" Noah asked.

"Pretty much."

"Wow, that's cool. How can Lucas and I help?"

"You already did by painting and sweeping and washing windows. Lucas has a part-time job on Saturday afternoons with me stocking the pantry."

Lucas looked up from his plate. "I do?"

"Yeah, you do," Rob said. "We talked about this, remember?"

"Oh, yeah. I forgot." He fiddled with his napkin. "What if I want to sign up for baseball?"

"The pantry will be open several days a week, Lucas. We'll find a shift that works. No worries."

"Can I help, too?" Noah asked.

"Sure, we'll put you to work, too," Rob said.

"Do we have time for another game of chess?" Lucas asked. He shot Rob a hopeful look.

Rob laughed. "Don't you think trouncing me once today is enough?"

"I'm getting pretty good, aren't I?" Lucas asked. His grin lit up his face.

"You are," Rob said. "Not pretty good. Very good."

Hannah listened to the conversation with a smile. It had become clear that the two were growing very close. The difference in Lucas's self-confidence was noticeable.

"It's late, Lucas," Hannah finally said. "And we have church in the morning. Put your dish in the sink and get cleaned up, please."

She looked at Noah. "You, too, pal."

"Night, Pastor Rob," Lucas said.

"Night, Lucas. Thanks for all your help today."

Noah slid his dish into the sudsy water, then stood next to Rob's chair. He put his small hand on Rob's arm and looked up at him. "Goodnight, Pastor Rob. I always pray for you at bedtime, and I thank God that you're our friend."

"Thanks so much, Noah." Rob covered the small hand with his own. "I thank God daily for you and your brother and your mom, too."

Noah smiled and nodded, pleased with the response.

Rob watched Noah leave the room. He looked up, his eyes tender as they met hers. "It was a good day," he said quietly.

"Yes, it was." Hannah sniffed, holding her emotions at

bay. There had been quite a few good days since Rob came to Tumbleweed. She wouldn't mind a few more.

"I should go," Rob said. He stood and stretched, then took his dish to the sink. "It really has been a long day, hasn't it?"

Hannah nodded. "I'm still pinching myself that the rummage sale exceeded all our expectations."

"Patty and Louise were right," Rob said. "Tumbleweed knows how to fundraise."

"Uh-huh. I'll be finalizing the grand opening plans this week. What do you think about an open house, say noon to four p.m.? I'll send out email invitations. And surely we can use the discretionary funds to actually pay Luna for dessert trays and beverages for the event."

"All of that sounds fine by me. I leave it in your hands. Or hand, since you still have a cast."

"I'm excited. I'll start making phone calls Monday."

"How about if I dry those dishes?" Rob said, glancing at the dish drainer.

"I have it on good authority that the kitchen police are not on patrol. I'm going to leave everything. We've done enough for one…make that two days."

"Okay. Sounds good." Rob stretched. "Boy, I am tired." Then he cocked his head. "Is that your phone or mine?"

"Do you hear a phone? I don't know. We left them both in the living room when you and the boys were playing chess."

"I'll check," Rob said. "Might be important."

"You're right. I can hear it now." Hannah followed him into the living room. It was his phone, on the coffee table, buzzing.

Rob scooped up the cell, frowning as he read the screen and took the call. "Hey, what's up?" He nodded a few times, then closed his eyes and paced back and forth.

Hannah tensed. Something was wrong. Very wrong.

"Montgomery? Got it. Right. Right. I'll be there immediately." He tucked the phone in his pocket and looked at her. Pain filled his eyes, while confusion and utter grief etched themselves on his face.

"You said 'Montgomery.' Was that the police chief, Daniel Montgomery?"

"Yeah. I mean, no," Rob said, his voice raw with emotion. "It was Jim Stewart." He took a deep breath. "Chief Montgomery's brother and sister-in-law were killed tonight by a drunk driver."

Hannah covered her mouth with her hand, biting back a sob. "They have little kids. Twins."

"Yeah. That's what Jim said. They weren't in the vehicle." Rob swallowed and released an agonized breath. "I've got to go be with the family."

"Of course. I'll reach out to Patty and Louise. They'll get the church ladies in motion and the prayer tree, too."

Rob put a hand on Hannah's shoulder. He leaned close and kissed the top of her head. "Thanks, Hannah. I know you'll explain to the boys."

"Yes, and I'll be praying for you, Rob."

He nodded and left.

For minutes, Hannah stood in the middle of the living room with her arms wrapped around herself, numb with the knowledge that this would be the most difficult thing Rob had to do since he came to Tumbleweed. Her heart hurt for a man who'd lost so much.

Yes, Rob Sterling knew loss and grief intimately. Tonight would crush him down to his soul.

"Lord," she whispered. "Be with Your servant."

Chapter Ten

Rob walked up the steps to the parsonage, his feet leaden, his heart aching. The air was thick with the sweet, almost sickly scent of hyacinth. Someone had planted the bulbs that had begun to emerge around the property. He preferred the smell of rosemary in the yard. Maybe he'd plant some if he stayed.

The creak of his porch swing had him stopping in his tracks. Though the yellow porch light was on, the juniper bushes hid part of the porch. A shadow cast on the house revealed that someone was there.

"Hello?" he called out.

"It's only me, Rob," Hannah said.

"Hannah, what are you doing here? It must be nearly dawn."

"I thought you might want to talk to someone. Your visit with the family had to be difficult."

He walked up the steps and leaned against the post. "Who's with the boys?"

"They're sleeping over at Luna's. I walked over."

"Hannah, you ought to be asleep now yourself. You've had a long day."

"You have, too."

"Yeah, but long days are part of my job. Sitting with patients in the hospital, comforting grieving families at night.

All part of the job description." He released a breath. "Not my favorite part, but it's essential."

She raised her slim shoulders and dropped them. "I couldn't sleep knowing that family was suffering. Knowing you were as well."

Rob looked away at her words. Tonight had been harder than anything he'd experienced since the fire that took his wife. So much pain.

He took a moment to compose himself.

"Do you want to come in?" he asked. "It's warm out here."

"No. Actually, the temperature has dropped. Besides, it's probably best if we sit outside or people will talk. You don't need that sort of gossip. Your ministry in this town is too valuable."

"Thank you for that," he said. "Mind if I take a spot next to you?"

She scooted over on the swing.

He eased down next to her and released a breath. "Ah, it feels good to sit."

For minutes they rocked slowly. The creak of the swing was a rhythmic sound in an otherwise silent night.

"Something like this makes you think, doesn't it?" he said. His voice sounded hoarse and rough to his own ears. He'd managed to keep it together for hours to comfort the two grieving families who, in their crisis, no doubt questioned the very foundation of their faith.

Now? Well, now he was exhausted as the cracks in his own foundation were exposed.

"Yes," Hannah said. "It can really rock our faith if we allow it to."

He could only nod as she said the words rolling through his own thoughts. *If we allow it to...*

Except for an occasional barking dog, Tumbleweed remained quiet. Not even a car engine could be heard on Main Street. His parishioners were probably asleep, anticipating church soon. Two families weren't asleep. No, they were holding each other close, grateful for their loved ones' promised eternity with the Lord, while coming to grips with the hole in their hearts.

For some reason, he couldn't compartmentalize tonight. It wasn't working. Everything that had been in neat drawers, tucked away carefully, was spilling out in a disorderly mess. He was more than confused, unable to make sense of what happened tonight, his thoughts ping-ponging to another time and another death that hadn't made sense.

The rational part of him knew things would be better after a good night's sleep. Right now, he couldn't sleep if he wanted to.

Yeah, he'd sleep tomorrow after services.

"Funny how we mere mortals like to believe we have it all together," Rob finally said. "But that implies that we're in control." He swallowed hard and swiped at his dry, gritty eyes. "No matter how prepared we are for our blessed eternity, death still comes in like a thief, taking us by surprise and knocking us to our knees."

Hannah took his hand and wove her fingers through his. "When is the funeral?"

"Wednesday. I'll do the service, of course." He looked down at their hands together, marveling that he was fortunate to have Hannah as his friend. If he was honest with himself, she'd become more than his friend. Hannah was his rock and confidante, a precious blessing that had only grown since he accepted the position here in Tumbleweed.

God knew about Hannah before Rob had signed the contract.

"Are you sure you don't want Sam to handle the funeral service? Everyone would understand."

"Would they?" he murmured.

"Yes."

They'd understand? How? Why? Because they knew he was a widower? He had often wondered exactly what the community knew about him. Through what lens had they viewed the newcomer to their town?

"What did the town grapevine have to say when I showed up in Tumbleweed?" he asked.

"The grapevine? Just the usual cute guy stuff." She smiled slightly. "Jim Stewart called a meeting of the church staff before you arrived. He explained that you lost your wife and unborn child in a terrible accident and asked us to be discerning in our discussions with you about the topic." She swallowed as though nervous.

"Jim told us that he'd known you a long time, and that he'd prayerfully asked the Lord to provide the right man for the position. According to him, that man was you."

Hannah looked at him, then continued. "I still recall his exact words. 'Rob Sterling has a heart for the Lord and would be an asset to our community.'" She nodded. "He wasn't wrong."

"Hannah, Jim was very gracious in his introduction. Too gracious. I don't deserve such generous words." He grimaced. "There's more to the story."

"What do you mean?" she whispered.

Rob looked at the questioning and compassionate expression in Hannah's eyes. He knew this moment was coming. That he'd have to talk about what happened. He'd been given a reprieve from his past since arriving in Tumbleweed.

As difficult as the last hours were with a grieving family, telling Hannah what he'd done would be much harder. But he'd prayed for the right opportunity. The right moment. Well, the door just opened. There was no good reason to delay the inevitable.

He eased his fingers from hers and rubbed his hands together, almost as though praying.

"I've come to realize how important you are to me, Hannah. I didn't expect or plan to care for you, but I do." He glanced at her and then away. "That said, it wouldn't be fair for me to let you believe I'm the man that you think I am."

"You *are* the man I believe you are. I have no doubts."

"Maybe you will." He took a deep breath. "You need all the facts to make that determination."

"I'm listening," she said.

Rob closed his eyes for a moment, working to find a way to tell his story. The unspeakable story he hadn't voiced in four years.

"After we got married, Cassidy and I left New Hampshire. I accepted a teaching position at a small Bible college in North Carolina. She taught at a nearby elementary school. We rented a house off campus. It was a quirky Victorian that was about one hundred years old. If Cassidy plugged in her hair dryer on the second floor, the kitchen lights would go out. Sometimes, there were noises in the night. We'd laugh and say the house was still settling, though we knew there were probably bats or squirrels in the attic."

He rubbed his chin with the back of his hand and forced himself to continue.

"We'd only been there a month. I had left a voicemail for the landlord, insisting that he have someone check the electrical and call an exterminator for the attic. Then I had to go out of town for a conference. We'd only recently done a home test and found out that Cassidy was six weeks pregnant. It should have been the most exciting time of our lives."

Should have been.

Rob stared out into the night, his jaw clenched, praying silently for the strength to continue. "I left for the conference on a Friday, spoke to her Friday night. In the middle of the night before dawn on Saturday, the wires shorted and started a fire. The neighbors called the fire department. Cass was overcome by smoke and never made it out."

"Oh, Rob." Her voice quivered. "I'm so sorry."

"I let her down. Plain and simple."

"Surely you know that it wasn't your fault. It was a horrible, horrible accident, which could have happened whether you were home or not."

"Yes. I understand the facts. I know all the right words. Words I would tell someone else in the same situation. That, too, is my job."

He closed his eyes and opened them. "I know in my head that sometimes there is no resolution. No closure. I know that we don't always get our questions answered to our satisfaction." Rob released a small sigh. "I'm trying to move on from those unanswered questions."

"That's why they call it faith. You know that as well."

He nodded. "The Lord has forgiven me. I need to forgive myself. I can recite a dozen Bible verses, but all I see in the mirror is the look on Cassidy's parents' faces. The accusation and the agony in their eyes. I see that—and my guilt—when I look in the mirror."

He shrugged as if pushing a weight off himself. "My in-laws sued the landlord. I didn't have the stomach for it. Then they donated the money from the case to a charitable education foundation in her name. That gave them a measure of comfort."

"Have you seen them since then?"

"Not since the funeral."

"You said Tom is Cassidy's brother. He's the one who's been reaching out to you."

"Yeah, he's reached out to me regularly the last four years. I haven't been able to face him until now. A conversation with Lucas helped me to see that I needed to change my thinking." He paused. "Tom deserves better. I invited him to come to Tumbleweed."

He turned his head and looked at Hannah. She seemed to glow in the golden light of the porch. Dear sweet Hannah. Was it wrong that he longed for something more?

Could she possibly feel the same way after what he had shared?

Hannah took his hand again. "This week is going to be especially challenging. But please know that I'm here for you."

"Thank you," he whispered.

"And Rob, nothing has changed between us. You are the man I think you are. I care for you, and that confuses me because I never imagined or wanted another chance to care for someone. Where do you and I go from here? I don't know. For now, I'm simply grateful to have you in my life."

Rob closed his eyes and swallowed. Mental and spiritual exhaustion washed over him along with relief. He and Hannah were okay, and she'd left the door open for something more between them.

That would have to be enough for now.

"This is for Pastor Rob," Luna said. She tucked a chocolate croissant into a white bag and slid it across the counter next to the bagel and chai tea Hannah had ordered. "We have a chocolate croissant agreement."

Hannah frowned. "A what?"

"All I am permitted to share is that it is a legally binding agreement. I can't tell you about it because it has to do with you, your broken wrist, and when you were snoring."

"What are you taking about? And I do not snore."

Luna raised a brow. "Sorry, girl, but you do."

"You scare me sometimes, Luna. Anyhow, he won't be in until this afternoon. This is the first time since he arrived in Tumbleweed that he's taken any time off. In seven months. That's quite a work ethic."

"Or quite a driven man." Luna shrugged. "Either way, it's about time. How's he doing?"

Hannah glanced around. Except for two high-school girls in the corner giggling as they looked at their phones, the shop was momentarily empty.

"I don't really know. I haven't spoken to him privately since Saturday. Tuesday was funeral preparations and Noah had a concert at school during the day, so I left work early. Wednesday, Rob left right after the funeral."

"This has to be devastating for him, in light of his history."

Hannah nodded and moved toward the cupcake display. She didn't want to talk about Rob behind his back. Or to casually chat about his pain. If there was one thing she'd come to understand on Saturday night, it was that she hadn't understood the depth of the burden Rob Sterling carried.

Now that she understood, it was almost as though she carried his burden as well. Where did that leave her? Hannah wasn't sure because what she had told Rob was true. She didn't want to love someone again. It hurt too much.

"Hannah?"

"Hmm?" She turned to see Luna looking at her with concern.

"Where were you just now?"

"What?"

"I was talking to you, and the next thing I know, you're somewhere else."

"Oh, Luna. I'm sorry. There's been so much going on. My mind is going in a thousand directions at full throttle."

"I understand. Let's start with the basics. How did the rummage sale turn out financially?"

"We met our goal and then some, thanks to people like you, Patty Wright, Jim Stewart, Mayor Louise, and dozens of other generous people in this town. I can't believe the pantry officially opens Monday. The day after Easter."

"I have it on the web page in bold font."

"Thank you." She gasped. "I need to place an order with you for the open house. I forgot to email it to you."

Hannah couldn't believe she forgot to place the bakery order. That wasn't like her. She prayed she hadn't forgotten anything else.

"Don't worry. There's plenty of time. What are you thinking?"

"Cookies. Twelve dozen. They're easy and don't require plates."

"That works. Oh, and by the way, I made bank Friday and Saturday as well, even with the discount I offered. Plenty of people told me they came because of the ad in their local paper. Having the sale between breakfast and lunch hours was genius. Shoppers were hungry, thirsty, and happy to buy."

"That's wonderful."

Luna nodded and smiled. "I love my job because I have ninety percent repeat customers, which is how I survive."

"I'm glad it was a profitable event for you as well. Patty Wright sold twenty-four of her pies. That's two hundred and forty cans of food."

"Amazing! Do you have shelving for all those cans?"

"Yes. I ordered them online. They were paid for courtesy

of the Big W Ranch and arrived last Monday. Rob and the boys put them together. Or so I was told. I haven't been allowed in the pantry building since I fell. Though I will admit to peeking in the windows whenever I stop into the bakery."

Luna laughed. "Good for Rob." She paused. "I just realized that you don't have a sign on the shop."

"Another thing I forgot. Rob wants an etched sign in the window. I haven't had a minute to check into it."

"I can help with that. I have a friend who has a friend. I'll get that taken care of Saturday."

"Saturday? On a holiday weekend?"

"I've been known to save the day with last-minute birthday or anniversary cakes. There are a few people out there who owe me favors. Big favors." She smiled. "I'll need the key."

"Text me when you need it and I'll bring it over." She looked at Luna. "Thank you for being such a wonderful friend."

"If you're feeling grateful, you can start working harder to find me a date," Luna said with a smile.

"Funny you should mention that. Rob's friend is coming to Tumbleweed."

"Now you're getting the hang of this. Friend of a friend. See how easy it is." She grinned. "Where's he from?"

"Humbolt, New Hampshire. Same as Rob."

"Another Yankee." She wrinkled her nose. "I guess I can't be too picky considering this town's lack of eligible men. I don't suppose his name is Prince Charming, is it?"

"Tom Archer. Rob was married to Tom's sister."

Luna's jaw slacked at the information. "Oh. That begs a thousand questions which will need answers."

"That I am *not* answering right now."

"Fine." She leaned against the counter. "Luna Perez Archer. I don't know. It lacks a certain *je ne sais quoi*. Of course,

I don't necessarily have to take his name." She tapped her chin with a finger. "But what about the children? Enrique and Jordana Archer."

"Stop that." Hannah laughed. "I don't have any details yet. He could be arriving next week or next month. I'll keep my ear to the ground."

"I'll expect nothing less."

"You and Roscoe are still coming for dinner on Sunday, right?"

"I'm looking forward to someone else cooking. What kind of cake do you want?"

"Chocolate?"

"Silly me. Why did I even ask? It's Rob's favorite." Luna crossed her arms and raised her brows. "Listen here, my friend. I think you've reached the point where you need to stop denying how you feel and admit that you're in love with the man."

Hannah's eyes widened, and she looked around the shop again. Leaning toward the counter, she lowered her voice. "I am *not* in love with him."

She stared at her friend, terrified Luna was right and that it was too late to do anything about it.

No. No. No. She couldn't be in love with him.

"Would it be such a horrible thing? Clearly, you care for him. What's your heart telling you, Hannah?"

"It's telling me that Rob Sterling is leaving town in September. What kind of fool would fall in love with a man who has one foot out the door."

Hannah feared *she* was that kind of fool.

Chapter Eleven

Rob parked his bike in the church parking lot and removed his helmet. For a moment, he sat on the motorcycle, bathing in the April sunlight. The first real sunshine in days.

The funeral yesterday had been rough. He couldn't help but see the parallel between the loss in the community and the somberness of Holy Week as each day moved them toward Easter Sunday.

Here it was Thursday already. He'd cleared his schedule today and planned only a few hours at work this afternoon to catch up on calls and paperwork. Early this morning he'd headed into Beaumont to get the proper license for the church van. Then, he'd taken a long ride on his bike through the countryside, stopping to enjoy the wildflowers, thinking about his time in Tumbleweed and what might lie ahead.

The drive had restored his spirit and filled the well. He was excited about giving the Sunday sermon again. Hope from despair wasn't a new theme, but it was universal. It was a reminder of eternal life and the promises of our God.

In the midst of the week's tragedies and the Holy Week journey to the cross, the resurrection waited. Good news from the grave. He could only pray that his words would reach the people intended to be touched by God's word.

Just then, Rob's cell phone beeped. Hannah had sent a call to his office voicemail.

Tom Archer. Rob listened to the voicemail, anxious and curious.

"Rob, I've decided to take you up on your offer. I know this is late notice but my schedule has changed. I've just landed in Houston. I don't want to inconvenience you but let me know if you're free today. I know the timing isn't ideal with the holiday and all. The company is working on a merger, so the schedule is somewhat out of my hands. I have meetings all day Friday and a tour of one of the satellite offices on Saturday. I fly out on Sunday evening, unless they decide they need me to stay. Anyhow, I'll call you when I get to my hotel."

There was a long pause. Then he heard, "It's been too long, Rob." Tom's voice broke for a moment, taking Rob off guard and setting off an ache in his heart.

He'd met Tom long before he started dating Cassidy. His best friend had been a casualty after the fire. That was wrong. A lot of things were wrong.

Rob sat frozen on his bike, stunned.

Tom Archer would be here. In Tumbleweed. For Easter weekend. The irony of the timing didn't escape him.

Well, this was it. No turning back now, pal. You invited him, and he's coming.

Way to rip off the bandage.

Rob had shared his heart and his past with Hannah, and now he would meet with Tom and ask his friend's forgiveness. Then, maybe he could finally move on from the past. He would always love Cassidy, but he sensed change was coming and he was more than ready.

The sound of pounding had Rob looking up. Helmet tucked under his arm, he moved to the walkway on the side of the church. A scaffold had been erected, and two men held a stained-glass window while Naomi watched at the bottom of a ladder and gave directions from the ground.

As he approached, she turned and smiled. "Pastor Rob. Good to see you. One window as promised."

Rob nodded. "I'm sorry we had to put you off a day. We had a funeral yesterday."

"I heard. I knew of the couple but never met them. Just terrible. I'm sorry for the congregation's loss. It's a loss to the community as a whole."

"Yes, ma'am, it is."

Naomi looked at him. "I checked my invoices. You paid for this window with your personal credit card." She cocked her head. "You are aware that insurance would have covered the damage."

"It was the right thing to do," Rob said. "Thank you for being discreet."

"Thank you for your generous and kind heart, pastor."

Rob nodded again.

"I believe you'll be pleasantly surprised when we get this installed. This design sort of got away from me. I've never had that happen before, and I can only assume that the good Lord had His hand in the project. So, when you see it, know that I'm the artist, but God is the architect. The final product is stunning, if I say so myself, and apparently I do."

"That's some endorsement."

She laughed. "I'm happy to give it as I truly believe this project was out of my hands."

"Thank you, Naomi."

"You are very welcome, Pastor Rob."

"I hope to see you on Sunday."

"Maybe." She grimaced. "I don't like crowds. Everyone seems to turn up at Easter and Christmas and then there's those cell phones that seem to go off." She shuddered. "I prefer the other fifty Sundays when it's the locals who know better. However, that said, while we were working I heard music from inside the building. I had the good fortune to observe Mr. Mattigan directing the children's choir. Meaning I snuck down the hall." She sighed. "I became a sloppy mess listening to their beautiful voices."

"So I may see you Sunday?" Rob raised his brows.

Naomi winked. "You never know. The Lord works in mysterious ways."

The voices of the children's choir filled the hallway with the chorus of Handel's *Messiah* when Rob opened the church door. Goose bumps ran over him.

It was a challenging choice for a children's choir, but that didn't stop Henry. Rob had no doubt the concert would melt the hardest heart come Easter Sunday.

Rob followed the music and stood outside the choir room, leaning against the wall, eyes closed, letting the praise music soothe his soul. After a few minutes, he pushed off the wall and headed to the kitchen for some coffee. The pot was full and smelled fresh. He filled his mug and went to the bulletin board.

God has the last word.

Five little words. Hannah was so very right. It didn't matter what he planned. God's plan was the period at the end of the sentence.

He stepped into his office and stopped. A chocolate croissant on a paper plate sat in the middle of his desk. "What's this?" he murmured.

"It wasn't me," Hannah said from behind him. "Luna sent it over. She claims you two have a binding agreement that has something to do with chocolate croissants."

He turned around and looked at Hannah for a long minute. Simply seeing her warmed his heart. She had no idea how she had saved him on Sunday morning. Simply allowing him to bare his soul changed him and he was grateful for her presence in his life.

"What?" Hannah asked. "Is there something on my face?" She touched her cheek, then wiped her mouth with her fingers.

"No. I'm just happy to see you. We haven't really talked since last Saturday." On Monday, the church was closed, and he'd spent most of the day in the pantry with Noah and Lucas. Tuesday had gone by in a blur. After the funeral, he sent everyone home, including Lester.

"You're right," she said. "It's been a busy week already. I'm digging out from everything. But at least the storage room is empty."

"I appreciate you, Hannah. You have a God-given gift of empathy."

"Thank you. That means a lot coming from you, Rob."

He glanced at her pink cast. "How's the arm?"

"Four more weeks if I behave. Since I'm banned from the pantry, I guess I'll continue to behave." She held up her hand, revealing a stack of pink messages in her fingers. "For you."

Rob took them from her, then flipped through the slips of paper. "Wow, what's going on?"

"The condensed version is that you have twenty-five invitations to Easter Sunday dinner. Most of them came through Monday and Tuesday, but I've only just gotten to the voicemails."

"No worries, but how do I handle the situation without offending anyone? I planned a nice quiet evening at home with a peanut butter sandwich and maybe an old movie."

"I suggest you tell them that you have already accepted an invitation to a delicious homemade Texas Easter supper at the home of a dear friend, in her modest but clean house in the country."

"I did?"

"Lucas and Noah and I hope you will." She smiled sweetly. "Luna will be there, too, and she's bringing rolls and cake. Chocolate cake."

"You should have led with that." Rob laughed. "I'd be honored to accept your invitation."

"We look forward to having you. Roscoe will be there, too. I hope you don't mind."

"Nah, he's okay, that dog." He looked at Hannah. "Do I have to call all twenty-five of these parishioners back?"

"I didn't want to presume, but I used to send regrets for our last pastor. He was also a bachelor and liked to take off with a fishing rod right after Easter service."

"Smart man." He handed her the stack. "Presume away."

"Oh, Sam called to confirm he's taking over Friday night service."

"Wonderful." He slipped behind his desk and smiled at the golden, flaky chocolate croissant before him. "How are the grand opening plans for the pantry going on your end?"

"I've emailed invitations to the Tumbleweed Community Church Board, the Tumbleweed Ladies' Auxiliary, and all the small business owners, farms, and ranches in the area. I even sent invitations to the other churches in the area. Nearly everyone confirmed that they'd be in attendance. And I've ordered refreshments from the bakery."

"How about if we meet at the pantry early on Monday morning to review everything one last time before the doors open?"

"You're actually going to let me in the store?"

"I've Hannah-proofed it. Luna has been by a few times with decorating stuff that she said you approved."

"My personal interior designer. I can't wait to see the finished product."

"I can't wait for you to see it. You know, we had a pizza celebration the other night, but things have been so chaotic I haven't had a moment to appreciate that we raised the funds to pay a loan for ten months of rent in two days. I need to let that sink in and give the Lord the thanks and praise He deserves."

"I couldn't agree more." She turned to leave and stopped. "I also didn't thank you properly for your care when I broke my wrist. Time just zips lately. Thank you."

"Anything for you, Hannah. And I agree. It seems like just days ago, you and I decided to team up to bring a community pantry to Tumbleweed. We make a good team, don't we?"

"We do," she murmured.

Rob smiled. "I'm going to make a phone call, and then I'm out of here again. I've had a change in plans. Tom Archer just arrived in Houston. I'm going to drive over and take him to dinner."

"Rob, that's wonderful. I'll be praying."

An hour later, Rob walked across the hotel lobby as Tom Archer approached, a smile on his face. "Rob, so good to see you."

"You, too, Tom. Real good." He offered his friend a handshake and a hug.

Tom's smile and his gestures reminded him of Cassidy. That took him by surprise, though there was no sadness in the realization. It was like coming home to the familiar. He'd missed Tom, and this reunion brought him a joy he didn't expect, along with an almost nostalgic sadness that he'd missed more than just his friend the past few years. Cass was gone, but there were still good things in Humbolt to connect with.

Could he possibly go back?

"How about if we grab a bite in the hotel restaurant?" Rob asked. "It's convenient and I know you'll want to crash after flying all day."

"Sure." Tom took a deep breath. "I can't believe I finally got a call back from you."

"I've been busy." To his credit, Tom didn't ask the obvious question. *Four years of busy, Rob?*

Once they were seated and placed their orders, Rob shot Tom a questioning look.

"What?"

"How are your folks?" Rob asked, though he was somewhat terrified of the answer.

"Nothing has changed. I'd like to be able to tell you that it has, but I'd be lying. They don't blame you, Rob. It was never about that. Cassidy's death was more than they could handle and you were a reminder of what happened. But I'm still your friend. That hasn't changed in four years."

Rob released a breath. "Thank you." The words humbled him. Tom was right, and it seemed the better friend.

"What about you, Rob? Are you smart enough to stop blaming yourself for what happened?"

He looked at Tom and the sincerity in his eyes. Shame threatened to flood him, but Rob pushed forward.

It was time to face the fears that had paralyzed him for four years.

"I came here today to ask for your forgiveness. I want to move on and I'm beginning to believe I might have a chance of doing so."

"Surely you see that holding onto the past negates what happened on the cross."

"I do. Yet, forgiveness has been elusive despite my faith."

"It starts with you. Cassidy would never want you to spend your life rebuking yourself over something that was not your fault. The best way you can honor her life is to live yours, Rob."

Honor her life. Rob closed his eyes for a moment, processing the words. He swallowed.

"Tell me something, Tom. Why didn't you let me know sooner that you were coming in today? "

"Truth be told, I figured you'd back out of meeting with me if I gave you advance notice." He wrapped a hand around his water glass. "Four years, Rob. I lost Cassidy, and then I lost you, too. I've really missed you, my friend."

Rob met his friend's gaze and nodded. "I didn't realize there was something missing in my life until I saw you across the room. It was like coming home. You're the brother my parents forgot to give me." He grinned.

"You sound happy," Tom said.

"You're right, I am. Things have changed and I've stopped running. I'm glad you kept calling. Thank you for not giving up on me."

"What changed?"

Rob looked out the hotel window. What changed? Hannah and Tumbleweed, Texas. How could he explain?

"I've been coasting since Cassidy died. The lights were on, but no one was home. Moving to Texas has given me reasons to want to start living again."

"I'm really glad, Rob."

Their server brought their meals so they stopped to pray and begin eating. After a few minutes Tom looked up.

"Your folks tell me you haven't been home since the accident."

"Yeah, that seemed awkward, too." Rob folded the napkin on his lap.

"So you're punishing your parents?"

"No. I paid for them to visit me in Raleigh, but I couldn't

come back to Humbolt. I didn't want to hurt your parents by being seen around town."

"They've recently moved to Florida. It was too painful for them to stay in Humbolt. Like I said, I get it. I understand. But in grieving for Cass, they've forgotten they have another child. It's been difficult for me."

"How can I help?"

"Come home. There are churches in Humbolt. You can find the same reasons to find purpose again back home. Your folks would love nothing more than to see you regularly. You know that."

"I'm obligated to stay here through September."

"A lot can change between now and then."

"It already has." Rob toyed with his fork.

"Will you pray about Humbolt?"

"Sure. I can do that for an old friend." He smiled. "Now, you can tell me your actual schedule."

"The merger is real. I'm part of the due diligence team. I'll be busy for the next two days. I fly home late Sunday night."

"Come to Tumbleweed for church. And I'm having Easter supper with friends. There's room at the table for one more."

"That would be nice. Yeah, sure. I look forward to it."

"As am I. All my friends at one table, celebrating the resurrection."

Hannah glanced around the sanctuary. Every pew was packed and there were people standing in the vestibule. The altar had been decorated with flowers provided by the Tumbleweed Ladies' Auxiliary. In the center of the altar a gold vase stood, with long-stemmed purple and pink flowers along with tall greens. Asian white lilies in pots with white bows lined the back of the chancel and added to the majestic celebration of the service.

Rob stood at the lectern, tall and straight, finishing his sermon. Pride swelled in her heart as he spoke. She sighed, knowing it was more than pride. She cared for the good-hearted pastor.

"He is not here, for He is risen, as He said. Come, see the place where the Lord lay." Rob closed his Bible and bowed his head for prayer, ending on a resounding amen.

Amens sounded across the sanctuary and the organ began to play the closing hymn.

Hannah took a deep breath. The sermon was nothing short of powerful, leaving her with the restoration and assurance she needed.

"Are we done?" Noah asked, tugging on the sleeve of Hannah's blouse.

"Yes. I know you're tired. You sang at two services. I'm so proud of you."

"Does that mean we can go home and eat now?"

"Try to be patient, Noah. Next week, you'll be back in Sunday school. Today is special because of choir."

Noah responded with a small groan.

"We'll greet some of our neighbors, and then we'll head home."

She turned to Lucas on her other side. "Ready?"

He nodded.

Hannah made her way to the vestibule with the boys, greeting parishioners. The light caught her eye, and she looked at the new window.

"Lucas, look up there."

His face lit up at the sight of the sun streaming through, illuminating all the colors of glass in the cross. Naomi had added more colors than the original glass window. The result was simply stunning.

She wasn't the only one who noticed. Other parishioners

stopped to marvel at the streams of colored light and point at the window.

"It's fixed," Noah said. "That cross is beautiful."

Then Rob was at their side, smiling. "If it hadn't been broken, we never would have gotten this one. It's ten times better than the other, isn't it, Lucas?"

The boy gave a shy smile. "Yes, sir."

"Funny, how the Lord does that," Rob said. "He takes what's broken and makes it better than new. Better than we could have imagined."

Hannah marveled at his words. Yes, that was exactly what the Lord had done and was doing in all of their lives.

Henry joined them and put a hand on Rob's shoulder. "You really outdid yourself, " he said. "That sermon certainly raised us up from the ashes, just as Isaiah 61:3 tells us. Well done, Pastor Rob. It's been a challenging week, and you lifted the load and reminded us of what unites us in our faith." He offered an emotional smile. "Thank you."

"That means a lot, Henry. Thanks."

"Is Tom still joining us for dinner?" Hannah asked when Henry strolled away.

"Yes. He came to the early service. I gave him directions to your place. I appreciate you welcoming him into your home." Rob hesitated. "I'm glad he came to Tumbleweed. The Lord has done a work in me with his presence." His voice held emotion as he said the words.

"I'm glad, Rob." She smiled. "But be warned, Luna is going to grill him like a summer barbecue."

Rob laughed. "I'll warn him. See you soon." He looked at Noah and Lucas. "Be sure to help your mom, boys."

"Yes, sir," her sons agreed in unison.

Hannah smiled as she watched Rob walk away.

* * *

"Not another question," Hannah whispered to Luna after Tom Archer arrived at her house a short while later. "He's only been here five minutes. I don't know any more about him than you do."

"Well, you know he's a gentleman. He brought that big bouquet of flowers for you."

"They're nice," Hannah admitted. She glanced over at the kitchen table where they sat in a crystal vase. It was a lovely gesture. She couldn't imagine where he'd gotten flowers on a Sunday, and admittedly the arrangement was stunning.

But she was partial to wildflowers. Especially bluebonnets.

"He's cute. And he talks just like Pastor Rob," Luna said. "With that cute Yankee accent. Not a single y'all in sight."

Hannah elbowed her friend. "We're in the kitchen washing lettuce. They're in the living room. Unless they're hard of hearing, they can hear you."

"No, they're so busy watching football, they won't give us a notice."

"I hope you're right."

"Tom wants to help with dinner, ladies," Rob called. "He thinks he's inconveniencing you."

Hannah went to the doorway of the living room, where all eyes were on the football game, and knocked on the doorframe.

"Thank you for offering, Tom. Any other time, I'd say yes, but there are certain rules we honor on Easter and Thanksgiving and Christmas." Hannah raised her index finger. "This is Texas. After we worship, we watch football. I'm not a fan. I leave that to the rest of you." She raised another finger. "I'm the boss of the kitchen, and you're not. So sit back and relax and leave the meal to me."

Luna laughed from behind her. "For the record, I'm not a fan of football, either. I like those soccer fellas in shorts."

"I appreciate the clarification, Luna." Tom winked. "And once again, Hannah, thank you again for welcoming me into your home on such short notice."

"My pleasure."

"He has a sense of humor. I like him already," Luna whispered. "Maybe we can convince him to stick around."

"Maybe you can," Hannah said.

For a moment, she eyed the two men in the living room, talking and laughing as they watched the game. Warmth filled her at the wide smile on Rob's face. He was happy and he deserved to be. Yet, a niggling something worried her. A something that warned her he might be leaving soon.

"What else can I do?" Luna asked.

Hannah turned to her friend. "You could take a peek at the ham and see if it needs a little aluminum foil on top? I hate when it overbrowns."

Luna grabbed an oven mitt and opened the oven door. The aroma of ham, cinnamon, and pineapple drifted into the room. "Nicely browned and that little thermometer has popped out."

"Then it's time to eat."

Hannah called the football fans to the table.

Once they were seated, she turned to her oldest son. "Lucas, would you please sit at the head of the table and say grace?"

"Aw, Mom. We have a pastor here. That's his job."

"He already did his job this morning. Twice. Now it's your turn."

Hands connected around the table and heads bowed. Lucas took a deep breath. "Lord, You are a guest at our table. Bless our food today. Thank You for everything You give us. Amen."

Seated next to Lucas, Rob reached out to put his hand over the boy's. "Nicely done."

Lucas nodded shyly.

"We stopped by your food pantry on the way here," Tom said. He smiled and accepted the bowl of mashed sweet potatoes handed to him.

"Wait," Hannah said. "I thought you gave him directions, Rob. I assumed it was a coincidence you showed up at the same time." She held up the ham platter while Noah put his fork in a slice and added it to his dinner plate.

"I'm notoriously bad with directions," Tom said. "And the car's GPS navigation kept directing me to the middle of a cattle field. I finally drove to town and called Rob for help."

Hannah smiled. "Your GPS wasn't too far off the mark. There is a cattle ranch on the other side of the property line. The Big W Ranch. The biggest spread in the county."

"Still, you have to admire a man who asks for help," Luna said. "Pass the butter beans, please, Lucas."

Rob started laughing at Luna's comment. "Luna is our local baker extraordinaire. Those rolls are her creation. She helped make the pantry a success."

"The pantry," Tom perked up. "That's what I was going to say. What a blessing to your town."

"Rob and Hannah's brainchild." Luna put her hand on her chin and gave Tom a thorough evaluation. "What brings you to Tumbleweed, Tom?"

"I'm a mortgage banker. Boring, I know." He eyed the basket of rolls Noah had handed to him and placed two on his plate.

"Not at all," Luna said. "I find you… I mean, *it*, fascinating."

Hannah kicked her under the table.

"Ouch!"

"Sorry about that, Luna," Hannah said.

"What brings a mortgage banker to Texas?" Luna continued.

"I'm assisting in due diligence. We've got a merger in the works." He smiled. "For the next few months, it means I can visit Tumbleweed more often. I love Texas. Especially your accents."

Hannah looked at Luna, whose lips were twitching. "That's funny," Hannah said. "Because we were saying earlier that we thought your accent was interesting."

"Do I have an accent?" Tom looked at Rob. "Nah. I talk like everyone else."

"You do," Rob said. "Trust me. Besides the accent, there's a whole different language here in Tumbleweed. I find myself saying words I didn't even know existed last year. They refer to soda as pop here. That one took me by surprise. Oh, and they call a bubbler a water fountain."

Lucas laughed at Rob's comment. "Pastor Rob, you called the church basement a down cellar the other day."

"That's what it is."

Lucas laughed even harder. "No, it's a basement. Right, Mom?"

"Lucas, that's the beauty of our country," Hannah said. "We are all correct."

"I suppose I should sign up for Texan 101," Tom said.

"I'd be more than willing to tutor you on how to talk like a Texan," Luna said.

"Thank you, Luna. Truth is, I'm trying to convince Rob to come back to Humbolt when his contract is up here. The pastor there is retiring, and he's willing to wait until fall if Rob is interested."

Hannah tensed, her jaw tightening at the words. Yes, of

course Rob would go back home to New Hampshire. This wasn't a surprise, was it?

This time Luna kicked Hannah and followed that up with a meaningful look that commanded her to speak up. Instead, Hannah worked to stay composed…and silent. She had told Luna Rob was leaving only a few days ago. Hannah refused to rise to the bait.

"Rob would be a blessing wherever the Lord leads him," she said.

"Seriously?" Luna mumbled. She made a choking sound and turned to Rob. "What are you going to do?"

Rob grimaced. "I promised Tom I'd pray about it, and I will."

"What's so great about New Hampshire, anyhow?" Luna pressed.

"Well, for one—"

Rob put a hand on Luna's arm. "September is a long way off."

"Is it?" Luna asked sweetly. "It can seem like a lifetime when you make the wrong decision."

As if sensing the tension, Tom looked at Lucas. "I hear you play chess very well."

The conversation soon turned to strategy, with Lucas chiming in about what Rob had taught him. When Tom suggested they play later, even Noah was eager to see a match.

While they talked chess, Hannah sent a silent warning to her friend to back off. Luna was the kind of friend everyone should have in their corner. However, she was also the friend most likely to start a brawl.

Hannah ate quietly, nodding and smiling as the table conversation swirled around her, her eyes focused on a loose thread in the pale-yellow jacquard table cloth. When she looked up, her gaze landed on the dinner plates, all pushed back slightly, with forks resting across them. Rob and Tom leaned back in their chairs, discussing the old days. Every now and then, Rob burst out laughing over something his friend said.

She'd never seen him laugh so much, and she certainly didn't have any old days with Rob. But she did have the last seven months, and they were the foundation for what she had come to believe might be a future for them.

Had she gotten it wrong?

Hannah sniffed the air. Coffee. Her eyes went to Luna. "Did you put on the coffee?" she asked quietly.

"Yes. You didn't even notice me slip away from the table," Luna murmured.

"All those carbs," Hannah said. "They made me sleepy."

"Oh, is *that* it?" It was clear from Luna's expression that she remained unconvinced.

"Why don't we clear the table and get dessert?" Hannah asked no one in particular.

"Did I hear dessert?" Tom asked. "Hannah, that was a delicious meal. I'm not sure I even have room for dessert after this feast."

"Don't worry about dessert, Tom. I'll eat your chocolate cake for you," Rob said.

"Chocolate cake. That's right." He grinned. "You said your favorite was on the menu."

"You should have seen the cake Miss Luna made for Pastor Rob's birthday last month," Lucas said. "There were truffles on top. I never even had a truffle before. It was the best cake ever."

"Aw, Lucas. Thank you," Luna said. "I'm glad someone appreciates my many talents."

Tom looked across the table at Rob. "Your birthday? That can't be right."

Hannah's gaze shot to Rob at the same time and she saw the silent communication between him and his old friend. Tom immediately nodded and fell silent.

When Luna got up, Rob raised a hand. "Sit, Luna. It's my turn to help."

Hannah sighed and nodded to Luna while putting yet another smile on her face. "Thank you, Rob. That's nice of you."

"Take your time," Luna said. "I'm going to find out more about good old New Hampshire." Luna scooted herself down to the chair next to Tom and offered him a saucy smile.

"I don't know if I should be flattered or concerned," Tom said. He glanced over at Roscoe slumbering in the corner. "You won't sic your dog on me if I say the wrong thing, will you?"

"No. Roscoe only eats people on Tuesdays." She looked at Noah and Lucas. "Right, boys?"

Noah giggled and Lucas tried not to laugh.

Rob carried a stack of plates to the kitchen, while Hannah grabbed the ham platter.

"Everything okay?" Rob asked as he placed the dishes on the counter. "Things got a little awkward in there for a minute."

"Luna's like everyone else in this town. She's come to see you as a native. You even talk like one of us now. We're protective of our people in Tumbleweed. No one wants to entertain the thought of someone who's added so much to our lives leaving us."

"Wow. That's the nicest thing you've ever said to me." He looked at her, long and hard.

"Is it? If so, I apologize because you should be told more often. You've enriched our days and blessed us. We'll all be sad when you leave."

Confusion flashed in his green eyes. "I didn't say I was leaving. I told him I'd pray about it."

Hannah shrugged. Yes, she knew what that meant.

There was unspoken meaning in many of the daily candid phrases she'd grown up with, such as "bless your heart," which amounted to a gentle insult. "All hat and no cattle" was another. Then there was "I'll pray about it." A kind way to avoid making a decision nobody would be pleased with.

She feared that was the case with Rob. He didn't want to offend anyone in Tumbleweed.

Hannah picked up a bundle of clean forks and napkins. "Would you bring these out to the dining room, please?"

"Sure." He hesitated. "Hannah, are we okay? You and me?"

"Wait. I forgot the knife." She opened the drawer, grabbed a cake knife, and handed it to him.

"Hannah," he repeated. "Are we okay?"

She picked up the three-layer chocolate cake and examined the rosettes on top and neat layers of raspberry jam peeking out from the layers.

"We're fine. Just fine."

Rob nodded, concern on his face.

Well, let him be concerned. She was plenty concerned, too.

Hannah followed him back into the dining room, smiling.

She *was* an optimist, despite Rob's words to the contrary, she reassured herself. An optimist who came prepared.

Prepared to have her heart broken.

Chapter Twelve

Rob parked his motorcycle at the church on Monday and walked across the parking lot to the crosswalk. From the other side of the street, he could see that the lights were on in the pantry, and the front door was open. Hannah moved about arranging boxes on a display in the front window.

As if she sensed him, she looked up. When he waved, she offered a short nod and a smile.

She'd been acting distant since Tom had come for Easter dinner yesterday, but he hadn't had time to figure out what was going on in her head.

Behind her, Luna put a cheerful tablecloth over the free-standing counter and began to arrange paper cups and napkins.

Traffic on Main Street cleared, and he started to walk across the street. The closer he got to the pantry, the more something on the window had him frowning. Had someone written on the glass? Then he realized what it was and laughed aloud.

Tumbleweed Community Church Pantry was etched into the window in a half-moon design. "This is awesome," he said out loud.

Luna and Hannah stepped outside and stood beside him on the sidewalk, admiring the window with him.

"What do you think?" Luna asked.

"I'm gobsmacked. How did this happen?"

"Hannah told me about your vision and I reached out to a friend of my friend."

"Thank you both."

As the morning wore on, Rob couldn't help but notice that Luna did most of the talking. Hannah seemed unusually subdued today. More evidence that something was bothering her.

He found her arranging cans on a shelf and approached. "Do you like the setup?"

"I like everything," she said. "You and Luna did a fantastic job."

"Mostly Luna," he replied.

"Well, the shop looks like one of those specialty food grocers you find in the city. I bet Paul over at the Grocery Hub will notice and spruce up his place when he sees this."

"We aren't competitors," Rob said. "This is a food pantry, not a grocery store."

"And this is Tumbleweed, not Humbolt. We're a different breed, and as you've discovered, we're highly competitive here in Texas."

Rob's mouth nearly dropped at the rebuke and he took a step back. "Point well taken, Hannah. I'll remember that."

Lucas called to her, and she stepped away to join her son at the counter. For minutes, Rob simply stared out the window, stunned at her response, so unlike the Hannah he'd come to care for.

The doors officially opened at noon, though they were technically open all day to clear out any lingering paint fumes. Community friends stopped by with gifts to celebrate the event.

Dixie from the *Gazette* brought a vintage wagon and parked it on the sidewalk with a pot of blooming purple flowers. Verbena, she advised him. A dozen bottles of sparkling cider were delivered with a congratulatory note from the Tumbleweed Ladies' Auxiliary. Luna poured cider for the guests, who mingled and chatted.

Rob glanced out the window when a truck tooted a familiar tune. Buddy Tippens Sr. drove by in his big tow truck, his head out the window, waving enthusiastically.

Five minutes later, Buddy stepped into the shop. "Pastor Rob, I saw the crowd and figured this was as good a time as any to talk to you."

"Hi Buddy, glad you could stop by for the grand opening."

"Is it the grand opening?" He laughed. "That's right. I saw it in the church bulletin. By the way, powerful sermon yesterday. Powerful. I took notes."

"Thank you."

Buddy waved a meaty hand. "Hold on. Hold on. That's not why I'm here. The church van."

"The van is fixed?"

"No, I'm sorry. It's a goner. May it rest in peace."

"What about the part you were waiting on?"

"Never arrived and we can't locate another. My boys hit half a dozen junk yards looking."

"That's too bad," Rob said.

"Not all bad," Buddy said. He gestured outside. "Look out the window over to the church parking lot."

Rob got closer to the window. "That's the loaner van. What does it say on the side?"

"Tumbleweed Community Church."

Rob stepped outside and admired the shiny silver van with regret. "Why does it have the church name on it?" His stomach lurched as dollar signs flashed through his mind. "A new van isn't in the church budget. We'd have to have two rummage sales to afford that beauty."

"No. You don't get it. It's yours. Well, the church's. I had a long talk with my cousin and told him this would be a great tax write-off. He agreed." Buddy chuckled. "In truth, I arm-wrestled him for it. The deal was that if I won, the church would get the van. If he won, he'd put it back on the lot."

"You won." Rob couldn't stop laughing. "Buddy, you're something else." He pumped the man's hand. "Thank you. I can't wait to announce this in church on Sunday. We'll have our webmaster put it on the web page and mention you and your cousin's dealership."

"I'd appreciate that, Pastor Rob. Thank you kindly."

Buddy's gaze followed a cowboy leaving the pantry with a pink-frosted cookie. "Those look tasty. Mind if I take one?"

"Take several. They're from the bakery next door. Best cookies in three counties."

"No kidding? I always buy the cinnamon rolls. Never tried her cookies. That good, huh?"

"Better than good."

Rob couldn't help but grin when he stepped back into the pantry. He looked around for Hannah to tell her the news about the van but couldn't find her. He could be imagining things, but the distance between them seemed to grow as the day wore on.

At 2:00 p.m., the mayor stopped by. With no microphone available, she just hollered for everyone to pipe down.

"On behalf of the Tumbleweed Community Church board of directors and the Tumbleweed Town Council, I want to say a big thank you to Pastor Rob for seeing this vision through," Louise began. "Of course, he's not alone. The fine citizens of Tumbleweed stepped up to get the job done. Y'all volunteered time, money, and talent to make this a success."

"I cleaned out my attic," someone yelled from the back.

Laughter rippled through the room.

Louise continued. "Again, thanks everyone, and let's have a special hallelujah shout-out to the Lord for bringing us Pastor Rob."

"Hallelujah!" The room erupted into applause.

Rob nodded and offered a thumbs up. When he spotted Hannah talking to Jim Stewart, he began to make his way toward them. Except, it seemed every time he'd finish talking to one guest, another offered congratulations and a hand shake.

Finally, he stood in front of Jim and Hannah.

"Pastor Rob, I was just telling Hannah here that there's a rumor going around that you're going to leave us come September."

"I don't listen to rumors, do you?" Rob asked.

"Normally, no. However when it involves things near and dear to my heart, I might be guilty of listening."

"What's near and dear to your heart, Jim?"

"The Tumbleweed Community Church," the businessman responded, his voice testy. "Look, I don't have time to beat around the bush. Are you staying or not?"

"I'm giving the option consideration and a lot of prayer."

Jim's face soured. "Nothing wrong with New Hampshire. Your folks have a terrific one-of-a-kind diner. Though personally I don't understand why someone would quit their profession with benefits and a pension. Point is, Humbolt is not Tumbleweed. Anyone can see that."

"Humbolt was not Tumbleweed" seemed to be the theme today. Rob shook his head.

"So, the rumor is I'm going back to New Hampshire, huh?" He glanced across the room to Luna, who chatted about the vintage decor with several women. No doubt, Luna was the source of the *tea*, as she called it.

"You aren't seriously considering it, are you?" Jim studied him, looking furious.

"I'm seriously considering everything right now. Moving back home has a lot of appeal, and for the record, my parents are happy. Money and benefits don't buy happi—"

"Oh, don't give me that malarkey," Jim interrupted. "Sure it does. Maybe I ought to make staying worth your while."

"How would you do that?"

Jim was very serious, but Rob had no intention of giving him an inch. Jim Stewart had big purse strings, but Rob meant it when he said money didn't buy happiness. He waited for the businessman to put his intentions out there. While Rob didn't play poker, he understood the value of a good poker face.

"By making you an offer too good to refuse."

"An offer?"

"Let me make this as plain as I can. If you sign a two-year contract, superseding the current one, I'll give the church the pantry building free and clear."

Rob jerked back at the words. Even Hannah appeared stunned.

"What do you mean, *give* it to us?"

"You give me a dollar, and I'll sell you the building. A done deal."

"I heard that," Patty Wright called. "You cannot offer Pastor Rob a contract without the board's approval. You know that, Jim." The rancher sauntered up to them. She took a bite of a cookie and examined the icing. "These are delicious."

"Patty, you know the board will approve it. They have nothing to lose, especially when one of the biggest donors in town cuts this deal. Bottom line is that we don't want to lose Pastor Rob. He was meant to be in this town. Any fool can see that."

Hands on hips, Patty shot Jim her best "I run the biggest cattle ranch in the county, do not give me guff" look.

"I will concede that you are correct on that point, Jim. We do not want to lose Pastor Rob. But even if the board does approve the contract, which they will, you cannot manipulate people like this."

Jim scrunched up his face like she was spewing nonsense. "Of course I can. I do it all the time. Just ask my daughter."

Patty rolled her eyes, which seemed to be her knee-jerk response to Jim.

"What do you say, Pastor Rob?" Jim continued.

"I'd like to think about it. Pray on it."

Jim blew out a breath of frustration. "Son, sometimes you just have to let go and trust the good Lord."

Rob frowned. "Meaning what?"

"The offer stands for twenty-four hours. Not a minute longer."

"Jim!" Patty sighed loudly. "I cannot believe you are doing this."

"I didn't get to owning half of this town by backing down. Twenty-four hours. That's my final offer." He gave a harrumph and walked away.

"Oh, that man." Patty put a hand on Rob's arm. "Pastor, you do what you are led to do. It's true you're the best thing that's happened to this town in a very long time, but I want you to be led by the Lord, not Jim Stewart."

He looked at Hannah, whose face revealed nothing. Then back to the Wright family matriarch.

"That's my plan, Patty. That's my plan."

"I thought Pastor Rob was coming over for dinner after the pantry closed," Lucas said.

"Plans change. We'll do it another time." Hannah put away the leftover ham from the grilled ham-and-cheese sandwiches she made and began to clean up the kitchen.

Would there be another time? In truth, she had planned to invite Rob to dinner tonight. That was before Tom mentioned Humbolt, and Jim offered him a building. She never got around to it on purpose. There was no point ignoring the inevitable. Rob was leaving. It would be best to start getting them used to the fact that he wasn't going to be around.

"But, Mom," Noah whined. "We want to play catch."

"I'll play catch with you," Hannah said.

"You? I dunno." He shook his head, confused. His face telegraphed that it was a terrible idea.

"You don't want to play catch with me?"

Awkward was written all over her youngest son's face. What to say without insulting Mom. She gave him credit for not saying the words out loud.

"Well?" she persisted.

"It sure is fun to play catch with Pastor Rob."

Hannah put her right hand on her hip and stared her son down. "Noah. I can be fun, too."

"But you have a cast on your wrist."

"That doesn't mean I can't play ball."

"If you say so," he muttered.

"Come on, boys, grab your equipment. We can get thirty minutes of catch in before the sun sets." She was going to be fun whether they liked it or not.

Hannah made a couple of tries at throwing the ball to Noah and Lucas before they called time out and came over to talk to her.

"Mom," Noah cried. "That one went in the pond. Now, we only have four balls left."

"I'm sorry. I'll focus." This was ridiculous. She'd played women's softball in college. Throwing a ball was not out of her skill set. Besides, she was right-handed. She just had a lot on her mind.

Lucas looked her in the eyes with a serious expression. "You gotta throw to our mitts, or we'll spend all our time chasing the ball in the grass. I'm supposed to catch it in this mitt right here." Lucas punched down the center of the leather with his other fist, his expression fierce.

"I'm sorry," she said. "I'll try to do better." She couldn't believe them. How was this supposed to be fun when they were so serious about everything?

When they were little, they would follow her around like she was perfect. Things had certainly changed in a few years.

"Maybe you could hit some grounders for us," Lucas said patiently. "Rob says we gotta learn to field grounders if we're gonna be good at baseball."

Rob says. Rob says.

"I thought you wanted to be good at chess."

Lucas laughed and effortlessly somersaulted across the grass. "I *am* good at chess. I'm the best player in the club now."

"You didn't tell me that. Congratulations, honey. I'm so proud of you."

"Thanks, Mom. I guess I forgot. I told Pastor Rob."

"That's nice," she muttered. "But I'm your mother."

"What did you say, Mom?"

"Nothing, Lucas. Get ready for the grounders."

Hannah used her left hand to toss a ball in the air and her right hand to hold the bat and swing at the ball. She made contact with a few. A very few.

"Nice effort, Mom," Lucas said in a slow voice, as though she was five years old. "A little more practice, and you'll get it."

Hannah looked at the darkening sky, grateful for the approaching sunset. "Let's call it a night. I'm sorry, boys. It's been a long week. I guess I'm tired."

"Can we watch television instead?" Noah asked.

"May we. The answer is no. You don't need more TV. Pop in a movie. A very short movie."

"Can… May we have cake with it? There's leftover cake in the fridge," Lucas said.

"Okay. A small piece."

"Thanks, Mom," Lucas said.

"Thanks, Mom," Noah echoed. He raced after his brother, stomping up the porch steps like a herd of hippos to reach the door first.

"I got it," Lucas said as he reached for the screen door.

"No, I got it!" Noah shouted louder.

"Boys! Stop, or you're both going to get it!"

The screen door slammed shut twice before silence ensued.

Patty Wright would be very unhappy if the boys caused her cattle to suddenly stampede.

Strolling up to the house, Hannah plopped down on the porch steps. When her phone buzzed, she glanced at the screen. A text from Rob. Do you want to take a spin in the new church van?

Hannah didn't answer. She was not at the beck and call of a man leaving in six, make that five, months. Yes, she was feeling a touch angry. There would be some praying for forgiveness tonight. For now, she decided to stew a bit.

Well, she'd called this one. Don't give your heart away, Hannah. That was her motto. What had she done?

The bigger picture was that this wasn't about her. More than herself, it was about the town. She couldn't believe he had such little loyalty to Tumbleweed. Who leaves Texas on purpose?

Another text came through. This time, Luna. Can you talk?

"Sure," she muttered and pressed Call.

"Not a good day," Luna observed.

"Did you call to cheer me up?" Hannah asked. "If so, you should try another strategy. I've already come to terms with the fact that I'm not a fun mom. I don't need any other negativity today."

"Hannah, I know better than to give you empty platitudes. We both know that today was not a good day."

"Tell me about it."

Luna laughed. "I just did."

"I've been thinking about what happened in the food pantry. Jim Stewart offered Rob an entire building, but he didn't even look tempted. Why? Because he's leaving in September."

"I've been thinking about it, too, and I don't like what went down. Even I found that suspicious." Luna huffed. "On top of that, I believe Rob thinks I'm the one who spilled the tea about the New Hampshire offer."

"Are you?"

"I am wounded. No, I am not. I'm pretty sure that one of your boys, probably Lucas, mentioned what Tom said at Easter dinner to someone at school on Monday. That little person told a big person, who told Henry. And so on."

"Wait. How does Henry fit into all of this?"

"He's in the gossip chain somehow. Remember how I planned to open the bakery on Monday to help with the pantry grand opening crowd?"

"Yes."

"After we set up the pantry, I went back to the bakery to check on my staff, and Henry came by for a cup of Earl Grey and a cherry scone and asked me about Rob and specifically Humbolt, New Hampshire. It was around 9:00 a.m. Peak cinnamon roll time."

"So basically, the entire town knows Rob has a job offer back home."

"In a word, definitely."

"I'm going to have to give my notice at the church."

"What? Why? You love your job."

"Luna, Rob is leaving."

"You don't know that for sure. Ask him, silly."

"No. I won't pressure him to make a decision that should be one hundred percent between him and God. I want Rob to do what he's supposed to do. All I'm saying is that I cannot spend the next six months working with a man I'm half in love with, knowing he's most likely leaving."

She was an optimist, but that would be sheer torture. They'd throw him a going-away party in September. He'd pack up his desk and drive away on his motorcycle with her broken heart in his backpack.

"Only half?"

"What?"

"You're only *half* in love with him?"

"That's your takeaway from all this? Luna, I'm serious. The sooner I turn in my two-week notice, the faster I can evaluate my situation and determine my next steps."

"So you're just going to quit?"

"I don't want to leave my job, but I have—"

"Mom, did you say you're going to quit your job?" Lucas spoke from behind her. "Does that mean we have to leave Tumbleweed?"

"I don't want to leave Tumbleweed," Noah sobbed.

Hannah turned around so fast she nearly dislocated her neck. The phone fell into the grass, and she scooped it up with her right hand. "Call you later, Luna."

She stood and raced into the house. Of course it was Lucas at the door overhearing her conversation. Lucas, the suspected tea spiller.

"What's the rule about eavesdropping on other people's conversations?" she asked firmly.

He swallowed and glanced away. "Don't do it because you might not like what you hear."

"That is correct."

As for Noah, Hannah tried not to laugh at the ring of chocolate around his mouth and the dab of frosting on his nose.

He stomped his feet. "I don't want to leave Tumbleweed. Pastor Rob and all my friends are here."

"I'm sorry that the two of you overheard that," Hannah said. "I take full responsibility. I should have had my private conversation in my room. However, what we say in this house stays in this house." She looked at them. "Not a word of my phone conversation will be repeated outside this house. Do you understand?"

Both boys nodded.

"Can you say it out loud, like you mean it?"

Lucas sighed, and they both said, "We both understand, Mom."

Hannah nodded her head. "I can tell you both this much: We are not leaving Tumbleweed."

That was the one thing she was sure of. The only thing. Hannah glanced outside into the night. She loved this house, the yard, and the pond. Loved the peace and quiet. Why, she was seriously thinking about getting the boys a dog.

Besides, she and the boys were part of Tumbleweed. This was her community. Maybe she'd have to commute or find a work-from-home position. Whatever it took, she'd do it.

"Are you sure?" Lucas asked.

She turned back to him. "The last time I checked, I'm still the mom. I said we are not leaving Tumbleweed, and I mean it. Now, please go get cleaned up and ready for bed."

"Yes, Mom," Lucas said.

Noah pouted and said nothing.

"Noah?"

"Yes, Mom." He stretched out the word *mom* and gave a dramatic sigh as he did an about-face.

"Noah?"

Her son turned around. "What?" He sniffed.

"Is there any chocolate cake left?"

"Uh-huh."

Good because she would need a lot to make it through the next twenty-four hours.

Chapter Thirteen

"I'm sorry to see you go, Tom," Rob said. They sat outside a coffee shop near his hotel in Houston, having coffee and pastries.

The Tuesday morning business crowd passed by, moving quickly down the sidewalk.

"Nice that I got an extra couple of days in town and drove around Houston. Terrible traffic. You have it right, living out in the country."

"Tumbleweed is nice."

"It is. I'll be back again soon, no doubt. I'd love to see more of the town."

"Two stoplights. You've seen it all. But they're really serious about their football. We can cheer on the local team."

"I'd like that." Tom finished off the last of his croissant. "This is good, but there's no comparison to the one you brought me Sunday from Luna's bakery. How'd you happen to have half a dozen croissants in your car on Easter?"

"Long story. Luna thinks she owes me. She doesn't. But who am I to judge if Luna Perez wants to give me chocolate croissants?"

"You're well-liked in Tumbleweed."

"Am I?"

"Yeah. I saw it while standing in the vestibule and on the church steps after service. Everyone had a good word to say.

Your community loves you." He paused. "I know I mentioned it before, but that was a beautiful sermon you gave. There's not a person that can't relate to that universal theme. I overheard someone say it's been a tough week for Tumbleweed. There was an accident, and the community lost two parishioners?"

"Yeah. Very hard week."

"Your sermon touched hurting hearts. I know it touched mine."

"A good sermon isn't mine. It belongs to the Lord."

"Ah, yes, but this is your calling, you know."

"You think so?"

"I know so." He sipped his coffee, looking at Rob.

"What is it?" Rob asked. "What's the question you're holding back?"

His friend took a deep breath and said, "You aren't going to take the position in Humbolt, are you? And I'm not sure why not. I mean, the vibe is similar. Small town. Small church. Loving community."

"I said that I'd pray and consider it." Rob ran his finger over the rim of his mug.

Tom smiled. "Yeah, I don't think so. I suspect your heart is here. Does she know you're in love with her?"

Rob looked at him. "Do I have a sign around my neck or something?"

Tom chuckled. "No, but come on. It's pretty obvious. Were you ever going to mention it to me?"

That was a hard question to answer, and there had been too many hard questions lately. Rob swallowed. But Tom deserved an honest answer.

"Probably not." He was silent for a long moment. "Not a day goes by that I don't think about Cassidy. Think about our love and what might have been. I didn't seek to fall in love with Hannah. I ran from it. But I told you when you arrived. I'm done running."

He blinked back the moisture in his eyes. "I'll always love your sister. She's part of who I am."

"I get it, Rob. I get it."

Once again, they were silent.

"Just be sure to bring Hannah and her boys up to Humbolt when you visit your parents. Do it soon, Rob. We both know that life is short. We don't know the day or the hour. Don't waste any more of yours on the past. You have a wonderful future ahead of you. I'm happy for you."

"I didn't realize that I needed to hear that you were okay with me and Hannah. But I guess I did." Rob took a deep breath and nodded. He knew what he had to do next, and the clock was ticking.

Traffic was congested as he drove straight from Houston to the church. As he walked from the church parking lot toward Jim Stewart's office, he took his good old time. There was no use getting there too early. Jim said twenty-four hours. He had plenty of time.

Rob stopped at the diner for a sweet tea in Hannah's honor. Greeted a few of the customers before he hit the sidewalk again, arriving at Jim's office with thirty minutes to go.

The receptionist asked him to take a seat, and he did. After ten minutes, his knee bobbed up and down nervously and then his foot tapped a rhythm on the floor while he watched the clock.

"Excuse me," he asked the receptionist. "Does Mr. Stewart know I'm here?"

"Yes, he's been on the phone with an important client. It will be just a few more minutes."

He checked his phone. Hannah had never responded to his text last night. Not a good sign.

Just then, Jim Stewart stood in the doorway of his office, grinning. "Pastor Rob. Come on in."

Rob stood, suddenly realizing Jim hadn't been on the phone with anyone. He'd made him wait on purpose—all part of his strategy.

It's a good thing Rob had a strategy as well. An endgame strategy.

Jim sat down behind his desk in a worn leather chair. It creaked when he sat back and put one leg over his knee.

"Trying to make an old cowboy sweat, are you?" he asked. "I wasn't sure you'd show up."

"No, I had a few things to do." Rob smiled and relaxed. Only a few more pieces left on the board. "I'd like to negotiate that offer."

"That so?" Jim said. "What part of the offer?"

"First, I want you to ask the church board to give Hannah a ten percent raise."

"Ten percent?" Jim's feet hit the floor. "You're killing me."

"Hannah has three jobs to make ends meet. At the church, she does the job of two people. The church is growing. It needs a receptionist. With Hannah there, you're saving money. Do the math."

"Think Patty will give me pushback if I put that request on the table?" Jim asked.

"I think this will be one of the rare times that you and Patty agree on something."

Jim nodded. "You're probably right. So you're agreeing to the new contract and ownership of the pantry?"

"Not yet. I said first. There's something else."

Jim groaned.

"I want the contract for three years, with annual cost of living raises."

"Fine." His gaze went to the clock. "But you're running out of time."

"That's it, sir." Rob stood and offered his hand to seal the deal.

Jim also stood and took Rob's hand. "I'll get a meeting scheduled immediately."

"Thank you. Let me know when the meeting is."

"I surely will." He looked at the big clock on the wall and chuckled. "Good timing."

"I thought so." Rob turned to leave and stopped. "Jim, why did you put that ridiculous rental agreement on the pantry to start with?"

"You mean ten months' rent up front?"

"That would be the one."

"Because I may be old, but I'm not an old fool. I wanted to help you see how much you needed that pantry. How much you mean to this community and how much it means to you." Jim looked at Rob. "It worked, didn't it? Pulled you out of your fog and put you back on the road again."

"That it did. Thanks, Jim."

"You weren't really considering moving back to Humbolt, were you? I mean, it's a great place to visit…but this is Texas. The Lone Star State. It doesn't get any better than Texas." Jim frowned. "Is there even a football team in New Hampshire?"

"Intercollegiate."

"I guess that's something, and something is better than nothing." He eyed Rob one more time, his expression making Rob a little nervous. Finally, he opened his mouth. "What about Hannah?"

"What about Hannah?"

"You're in love with her. What are you going to do about it?"

Rob stared at him without words. So much for the poker face strategy.

"Look, son, let me give you the advice my granddaddy

gave me. Life isn't neat with a bow tied on top. We don't always get our questions answered, and sometimes nothing makes sense. Sometimes, you just gotta go with your gut. Like I said in the pantry yesterday. Let go and trust the Lord."

"Sir?" Rob frowned. This situation was reminiscent of his conversation with Lucas when he threw the rock in the window. He hoped Lucas wasn't as confused as Rob was right now.

"I'm telling you that you best figure things out fast before the opportunity walks away."

"You should know that this topic is not my area of expertise."

"What? Women?" Jim laughed. "You'll be happy to know that you are not alone. I'm old enough to know better, and I've never figured out how to keep my foot out of my mouth around members of the opposite sex."

Rob didn't know if he should laugh or not. "Thank you for that sage advice. If I figure things out, you'll be the first to know."

The sun was shining when he left Jim's office. Rob stood at the intersection of Main Street and Center Street, waiting for the light to change. He took a deep breath. They were mowing grass at the high school. Nothing like the smell of freshly cut grass. The light changed, and he crossed the street. A horn tooted, and when he looked up, Mayor Louise waved at him from behind the wheel of her pink pickup truck.

"Hey, Pastor Rob," she called.

He waved back. "Hey, Louise."

Then, from behind him, someone said, "Howdy, Pastor Rob."

Rob turned and smiled. "Hi, Mike. Nice day, isn't it?"

"Yes, sir. Sure is."

Mike Newton. Married to Stephanie. Three children. Rob grinned.

"Thank you, Lord, for all You have given me," he said softly.

At the park, he cut through on the pedestrian path to the church's back door. He checked his phone as he opened the door. The day had sped by.

He'd only seen Hannah in passing when he came in. Then he'd taken off for Houston and coffee with Tom.

Hannah had handed him his voicemails from the weekend and said she had an appointment to attend to and would be back later to catch up on her paperwork.

The building was quiet. The school bus hadn't been by to drop Noah and Lucas off yet.

He headed to the kitchen first. The coffeepot was unplugged, so he grabbed a water bottle from the fridge. Then he checked the bulletin board to read Hannah's latest quote.

But the board was empty.

Six months. No, it was now more like seven months in Tumbleweed, and in all that time, the board had never been without a quote. Sometimes, she put up the white index card with pithy, amusing or thoughtful quotes daily or when things were busy, weekly. But there was always something on the board.

Not today. Something was very wrong.

Rob headed to his office. He rounded the corner of his desk and sat down. A plain white envelope sat in the middle of his desk.

Dear Pastor Rob, I am writing to resign from my position as secretary at Tumbleweed Community Church. My last day will be April twenty-first.

Rob skimmed the letter with disbelief as it delivered a sucker punch. He whooshed out a breath of air.

Thank you for your support during this time. Hannah Bryant.

A resignation and two weeks' notice.

Rob took off his glasses and rubbed his eyes. His chest hurt and his head pounded.

He'd read the situation wrong at every turn. Messed up big time.

He cared… No, he *loved* Hannah and thought they were about to face the future together. The last seven months, they'd weathered so much. Together.

Things were falling into place.

Apparently, she hadn't gotten the memo. That was his fault as well. Twice in two weeks, Jim Stewart was right. Patty would get a kick out of that.

"You best figure things out fast before the opportunity walks away." Rob repeated the words.

He'd been so busy apologizing for a past the Lord had already forgiven him for that he'd completely missed the turnoff to his future. He hadn't even bothered to give Hannah his travel plans. She needed to know how he felt, not what his excuses were.

Not why he wasn't worthy of her.

Tom's words gave him pause. He'd been negating the cross and wasting valuable time to boot.

"I am worthy," he said aloud.

The church doors opened and slammed shut. Noah and Lucas raced down the hall. They quieted and slowed outside the offices, then sped up again until they reached the kitchen. Noah popped his head into the office and whispered loudly. "Hi, Pastor Rob. We got out school early today."

"Hi, Noah," he whispered back.

He'd never see the boys after school again. No more cookies and milk. No more chess or tossing the ball.

His heart was being ripped out of his chest. No more Hannah in his life. He grimaced as though in actual pain.

Rob picked up his phone. He opened his photo app. For minutes, he flipped through the pictures of bluebonnets and Hannah.

So what was he going to do about it? He refused to go out without a fight. And if he lost, then he'd at least know that he tried.

A glance at the clock on the wall said the bakery was closed. He called Luna, praying she'd answer.

"Pastor Rob, to what do I owe this honor?"

"I'm in big trouble."

"You called to tell me something I already know? And for the record, I did not spill the tea on the whole Humbolt-gate thing."

He couldn't help but laugh. "Humbolt-gate?"

"It's all anyone is talking about in the bakery. Frankly, I am tired of hearing about Humbolt, New Hampshire. They're doing internet searches on the town and the demographics. I think some of these women are seriously considering following you there."

"I'm going to fix that."

"Can you?"

"Yes, but I need your help."

"Say the word. I am all in."

"Will you watch the boys for a bit?"

"Define a bit. I'll need more information on the op if you want my help."

"A bit is as long as it takes to grovel and convince Hannah that I love her and want to spend the rest of my life with her."

He heard a crash as though the phone dropped. "Luna?"

"Sorry, I should have had a warning before you said that. I'm at the Grocery Spot and I dropped the phone in my grocery cart."

"Sorry about that."

"Oh, my word. Give me a moment to catch my breath. I nearly hyperventilated. I have one question. Do you want to spend the rest of your life with Hannah in Tumbleweed, or Humbolt?"

"Tumbleweed, Luna."

"Aw, this is so sweet. I love men who grovel."

"I'll meet you at the crosswalk with Lucas and Noah. Make sure they do their homework and don't eat too much sugar."

"Sure, give me ten minutes to check out with my groceries."

"I'm sorry to impose like this but I'm running out of time and opportunity."

"You sure are. Have you got a plan? Because this is going to take some finesse."

"I'm a pastor. I know finesse."

Luna laughed. "I sure hope so. See you at the crosswalk in ten minutes."

"Thanks, Luna. I appreciate you."

"I should hope so. I'll be praying for you, Pastor Rob."

"Thanks. I can use all the prayers I can get." An understatement at best. Could he convince Hannah that they had a future together?

The church offices were oddly quiet when Hannah returned. Rob was stealthy but she expected to hear noise from Lucas and Noah. She peeked her head into Rob's office. Her envelope was missing from his desk. Hannah swallowed. Oh, boy, this was going to be a lot more difficult than she anticipated. Two weeks until her last day. How was she going to last until then without crying or making a fool of herself?

She kept walking down the hall expecting to hear giggling. The kitchen was empty. She stood in the doorway, then turned and raced down the hall and peeked into her office. "Lucas? Noah?"

"Luna took them to the Friendly Fork for a snack."

Hannah whirled around at the sound of Rob's voice behind her. Hands in his pockets, he looked as sad as she felt.

"She didn't text me." Her phone suddenly beeped. "Oh, there it is." She gave a small embarrassed laugh. "Thank you."

This was awkward. He must have read her resignation letter by now.

"Well, um…if you'll excuse me."

"Do you have a minute?"

"If this is about my resignation letter, could we please have my exit interview another time? I'm exhausted. The last two weeks have been emotionally draining. I'll check your calendar and find a time on your schedule tomorrow. Will that work?" She looked everywhere but at him.

All she wanted was to go home and have a good cry. Was that too much to ask?

"I'm not asking for an exit interview," Rob said softly.

"Then what?"

"Could we please talk in the kitchen?"

"I guess so." She followed him down the hall, her stomach queasy, her legs heavy, as though she was walking the plank.

They entered the kitchen and Rob nodded toward the table.

"Have a seat." He paused. "I mean, *please* have a seat. And let me be very clear. You don't have to talk with me. You can leave at any time."

She sighed, pulled out a chair and sat down. Now she knew where Noah got his dramatic sighs from. His momma.

"I don't want to put you on the spot," Rob said. "But I hoped we could talk about how you got to here. Not about the job."

That was an excellent topic. One that she did not want to talk about. At all.

"Would that be okay?" he asked. "I can stop by your house, but that would be even more awkward with the boys around."

He looked at her and fiddled with his glasses. Rob seemed nervous. That sort of surprised her. After all, she was the one who'd made the premature assumptions.

"There's really not much to say," she said. "I foolishly thought that we had an understanding. That we were on the same page. Now I realize we are not. I'm extremely embarrassed for reading the situation wrong and I hope I haven't embarrassed you. I never wanted to be one of those Pastor Rob groupies."

He blinked with surprise. "I have groupies?"

"You do. I'm the gatekeeper around here, so trust me. There are groupies. Lots of groupies."

"I had no idea."

Hannah nodded, her gaze everywhere but in his direction. "Is that all? Once again, I apologize. I think it would be best for me to leave." She paused, searching for the words. This was humiliating. "I'll find a suitable replacement for the rest of your tenure here in Tumbleweed."

"My contract has been extended," he said.

"What?" She inhaled sharply and turned to look at him, "How? You rebuffed Jim's offer yesterday."

"I often am misjudged because I'm a pastor. I can be a little manipulating myself, when necessary. In this instance, it was necessary."

"You? Mild-mannered Clark Kent? I doubt it."

"Clark Kent?" He laughed. "I'm finding out all sorts of interesting *tea* today."

Hannah's lips twitched.

"I wasn't going to admit to Jim that I planned to stay in Tumbleweed because I wanted a better deal."

"But what about Tom?"

"What about Tom? It was great to see him and get things sorted out in my head and my heart. I hope to keep in contact with him."

"He wants you to move back home. You said you'd pray on it."

He raised his palms in gesture. "The truth is, I've been praying about my future for weeks."

"You really were praying about it?"

Rob stared at her and then started laughing.

"What's so funny?" she asked.

"You thought I was fibbing about praying?"

Hannah squirmed. "No. I thought you were trying to avoid hurting anyone's feelings."

"Maybe I was. After all, it was the first time I'd seen Tom since Cassidy died. I didn't have the heart to shoot him down."

"What about Jim Stewart? Why didn't you jump at his offer?"

"Patty Wright was correct. Jim shouldn't manipulate people. If I'm going to stay in Tumbleweed, it will be because I'm supposed to be here."

"And are you?"

"Yes. I waited until the eleventh hour to go to Jim's office. I agreed to buy the building for a dollar and sign a three-year contract on one condition." He looked at her. "That he give you a ten percent raise. He agreed to get the board to approve my stipulation."

"You bought the building?" Hannah nearly gasped aloud. "Wait. You said three-year contract?"

"I did. And a raise for you. Did you miss that part?"

"No. I'm still processing." She couldn't help but stare at Rob. Where was all this going? That voice in her head piped up. *Yeah, when is the other shoe going to drop?*

Hannah kicked the thought to the ground.

"So you're staying." Hannah worked to keep her voice even.

"Yeah. I am. Even Tom figured that out." Rob cleared his throat. "I noticed the quote is missing from the bulletin board today."

She shrugged. "There didn't seem to be much point. My optimism apparently does have limits."

"You don't have to pretend with me, Hannah." He smiled. "I found out the day we were stuck on the side of the road who the real you is. You're scared like the rest of us. Terrified, even." He adjusted his glasses. "That was a good day. I'm pretty sure that's when I fell in love with you."

Her eyes popped wide, because *she* was pretty sure that was when she fell in love with him, too.

Hannah looked into his eyes, and was startled to see the pain and sadness were gone, replaced by something else.

Her heart hammered.

What she saw was hope and love. Love shone in his green eyes.

"Now about that bulletin board," Rob said. "I took the liberty of putting up my own quote."

> My most brilliant achievement was my ability to be able to persuade my wife to marry me.
> —Winston Churchill

She frowned, confused as he recited the words.

"What does that mean?" she asked.

"Hannah, I made the decision to go out fighting. I don't want to pressure you. But I also don't want to spend the rest of my life wondering *what if*. What if I had the courage to tell an amazing woman I love her and I want to spend the rest of my life with her?"

Hannah was so surprised that she found herself unable to put words together. Instead, her eyes filled with moisture and everything became blurry.

Could this possibly be true?

"Hey, hey. Don't cry." Rob rushed to the sink and brought

her a paper towel. You aren't supposed to cry when I tell you I love you."

She blotted her eyes and took a breath. "I love you, Rob. I'm a little terrified at how much I love you."

"We can work on that." He nodded with a grin. "But this is good. Going much better than I thought it would."

"I can't say yes to marriage until I ask the boys, though."

"May I kiss you without their permission?"

Hannah laughed. "Please do."

Rob got up and came around the table. He took her hand, pulled her up and gently put his arms around her in a warm embrace. When his lips touched hers Hannah wondered why she'd waited so long to tell him how she felt.

The back door of the church burst open with an echoing thud. Startled, Rob and Hannah jumped apart.

Thundering down the hall, the boys raced into the kitchen with Luna behind them, carrying a bakery box.

"Did she say yes?" Noah asked.

Lucas stood next to his brother, his gaze going from Rob to her with concern.

"You told the boys?" Hannah looked at Rob, her face heating up.

"Of course not. I thought you were going to say no."

"You did?" She frowned and turned to look at Lucas, Noah and Luna.

Luna raised her hand and wiggled her fingers. "I told them."

"Luna!" Rob and Hannah admonished at the same time.

"Oh, come on. I knew you were going to say yes to Clark Kent."

"She calls me Clark Kent, too?" Rob laughed and adjusted his glasses.

"We're the only ones," Luna said. "Promise."

"Does that mean Superman is going to be our second dad?" Noah asked.

"What do you think, Lucas? Would that be okay with you?" Hannah asked.

"Yeah. That would be real okay, but I don't want to leave Tumbleweed. I don't want to move to Humbolt, New Hampshire. I looked it up. It's okay, but they don't have a football team."

"Yeah. No football team," Noah repeated.

"Y'all are funny." Rob laughed. "Are you sure you weren't talking to Jim Stewart?"

Hannah's jaw dropped. "You just said y'all!"

"Did I? Looks like we have to stay in Tumbleweed."

Hannah grinned. "He's correct. We aren't going to leave Tumbleweed. I promised and I mean it. Pastor Rob, I mean, Rob is staying, too."

"So we don't have to play catch with Mom anymore?" Noah asked.

Rob burst out laughing, then pulled a straight face. "Sorry, I didn't mean to laugh."

"It's okay. I admit it. My pitching arm needs work. I tossed a ball in the pond, too."

"We'll buy more baseballs," Rob said.

"Are we going to be a family?" Noah asked. He cocked his head and looked from Hannah to Rob.

"We are," Hannah said.

Luna sighed. "I love happy endings." She handed Rob the box in her hands. "Chocolate croissants. It appears that my work here is done. You two give me a call when you're ready to talk wedding cakes."

"Oh, Luna," Hannah said. "The maid of honor shouldn't bake the wedding cake. You'll have too much work to do running things."

"Maid of honor?" She hugged Hannah. "I do. I mean, I would be honored to stand up with you. Any idea when the big day will be?"

Hanna looked at Rob. When he nodded, she was certain he had read her mind.

"Soon," she said.

"I haven't bought the engagement ring yet," Rob said. "But we'll get it done once Hannah's cast comes off."

Luna gave a wave and skipped down the hall and out the door.

Rob chuckled. "I have a great idea." He turned to Hannah. "How about if we tear up your resignation letter and take a ride in the new church van. Then we can go to the diner for burgers and fries. Since this is a special occasion."

"What do you say, boys?" Hannah asked.

"Yes!" Lucas shot his fist in the air.

"Shotgun," Noah called.

Hannah laughed. "Sorry, buddy. Mom has shotgun."

The boys raced off down the hallway, their steps echoing as they departed.

Rob glanced down the hall to be sure they were around the corner. He looped his arm around Hannah's waist and pulled her back into the kitchen for a moment, resting his forehead against hers.

"I love you, Hannah," he said softly against her mouth.

"I love you, too, Rob." She looked into his eyes and laid a hand on his cheek. "Can this be real? You and I both get a second chance at love?"

"It's real, dear Hannah."

His lips captured hers and she said a prayer of thanks for all she'd been blessed with in Tumbleweed, Texas.

* * * * *

Dear Reader,

Welcome back to Tumbleweed, Texas. This is my first visit to Texas through my writing, and what a kick it was to research the people and land of this great state and their proud heritage. From sweet tea and barbecue to bluebonnets and endless blue skies, what's not to love about the Lone Star State?

The second book in this series is based on Hebrews 12:1.

"Wherefore seeing we also are compassed about with so great a cloud of witnesses, let us lay aside every weight, and the sin which doth so easily beset us, and let us run with patience the race that is set before us."

This is a story of never giving up, of patience, and of getting rid of the stuff that keeps us from achieving God's plan for us. For Hannah, that was letting go of control and embracing trust; for Rob, it was releasing guilt and accepting God's forgiveness.

Hannah and Rob have a special place in my heart. I hope you'll find that you can relate to their race and that you, too, find rest in God's unconditional love.

Please do email me and let me know your thoughts. I can be reached through my website, www.tinaradcliffe.com.

PS: Be sure to pick up the next book in the Tumbleweed series, by Mindy Obenhaus, *The Police Chief's Instant Family.*

Happy Reading!

Sincerely,
Tina Radcliffe